"Do I know the whole truth now?" Blu demanded. "Everything?"

The question had Kristen wringing her hands. All she wanted to do was go to him and curl up in his strong arms. But would he still want her once he knew *everything*?

She turned away. A moment later, his hand was on her shoulder. "What else, angel? What's so bad that you can't tell me, can't even look at me?"

Kristen felt him move close and, with easy familiarity, wrap his arm around her. Then his heat surrounded her, and memories of last night's passion flooded her senses. She squeezed her eyes shut, knowing she had no right to love Blu Dufray, to want him this badly.

He bent his head. "I'll help you, no matter what. Nothing you can say will make me walk away."

Kristen turned in his arms and gazed up at him. "Are you sure...?" she whispered.

Dear Reader,

Once again, Silhouette Intimate Moments brings you six exciting romances, a perfect excuse to take a break and read to your heart's content. Start off with *Heart of a Hero,* the latest in award-winning Marie Ferrarella's CHILDFINDERS, INC. miniseries. You'll be on the edge of your seat as you root for the heroine to find her missing son—and discover true love along the way. Then check out the newest of our FIRSTBORN SONS, *Born Brave,* by Ruth Wind, another of the award winners who make Intimate Moments so great every month. In Officer Hawk Stone you'll discover a hero any woman—and that includes our heroine!—would fall in love with.

Cassidy and the Princess, the latest from Patricia Potter, is a gripping story of a true princess of the ice and the hero who lures her in from the cold. With *Hard To Handle,* mistress of sensuality Kylie Brant begins CHARMED AND DANGEROUS, a trilogy about three irresistible heroes and the heroines lucky enough to land them. Be sure to look for her again next month, when she takes a different tack and contributes our FIRSTBORN SONS title. Round out the month with new titles from up-and-comers Shelley Cooper, whose *Promises, Promises* offers a new twist on the pregnant-heroine plot, and Wendy Rosnau, who tells a terrific amnesia story in *The Right Side of the Law.*

And, of course, come back again next month, when the romantic roller-coaster ride continues with six more of the most exciting romances around.

Enjoy!

Leslie J. Wainger
Executive Senior Editor

Please address questions and book requests to:
Silhouette Reader Service
U.S.: 3010 Walden Ave., P.O. Box 1325, Buffalo, NY 14269
Canadian: P.O. Box 609, Fort Erie, Ont. L2A 5X3

The Right Side of the Law

WENDY ROSNAU

Silhouette®

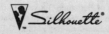

INTIMATE MOMENTS™

Published by Silhouette Books

America's Publisher of Contemporary Romance

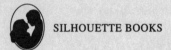

SILHOUETTE BOOKS

ISBN 0-373-27180-8

THE RIGHT SIDE OF THE LAW

This edition published by arrangement with Harlequin Books S.A.

Visit Silhouette at www.eHarlequin.com

Printed in U.S.A.

Books by Wendy Rosnau

Silhouette Intimate Moments

The Long Hot Summer #996
A Younger Woman #1074
The Right Side of the Law #1110

WENDY ROSNAU

resides on sixty secluded acres in the northwoods of Minnesota with her husband and their two energetic teenagers. A former hairdresser, today she divides her time between the family-owned bookstore, writing romantic suspense and traveling to locations for prospective books.

Her first book, *The Long Hot Summer,* was a *Romantic Times Magazine* nominee for Best First Series Romance of 2000.

Wendy loves to hear from her readers. Write to her at P.O. Box 441, Brainerd, Minnesota 56401. Or e-mail her at cattales@brainerd.net.

To Jenni,
for her amazing strength and wisdom,
and for her youthful energy and blunt honesty—
every mother should know when she's wearing
ugly shoes and the wrong color lipstick. And because,
as favorites go, you like this one best.
Always, with love...

Chapter 1

Salvador Maland pulled back the white satin sheet and slipped into bed next to his wife. When he focused on the nightgown that covered her nakedness, he said only one word. "Why?"

"Amanda's cutting another tooth," Kristen carefully reminded him. "If she needs me tonight, I want to be able to go to her quickly."

It was a viable excuse, one Salva couldn't contest. Everyone knew their daughter had been fussy for the past two days; it was amazing how a tiny two-and-a-half-year-old could disrupt even the most rigid of households. And the Maland home, located on a small island in the Caribbean just off the coast of Belize, was the most well-guarded, efficiently run home Kristen had ever seen.

"Then this isn't about this morning. You're not punishing me, are you? Because if that's what this is about, I swear—"

"It's not," Kristen assured, though Salva's cruelty before dawn had made her final decision easier.

She was so tired. Tired of being afraid. Tired of being on her best behavior *or else*. Tired of asking herself the same questions over and over again—such as who *was* this man who claimed to be her husband? And why had she agreed to marry a man she couldn't remember falling in love with?

But if she knew that, she would also know the standard information a healthy mind takes for granted. She would know her own birthday and remember her parent's faces. She would know where she'd grown up, and if she'd shared her childhood with other siblings.

Oh, Salva had given her answers. Three years ago, when she'd opened her eyes and found herself naked in his huge brass bed, he'd assured her that there was nothing to worry about; she was safe, at home with her loving husband. Then he had filled in the blanks: she was Kristen Harris from St. Petersburg, Florida. She was twenty-one, and as far as he knew, she had no family. He suspected her real name wasn't Harris, he told her, because she had been eluding the police at the time they'd met.

That particular news had shocked her, and seeing that it had, Salva had patted her hand and assured her that whatever mistakes she'd made were unimportant. That he and the island were her future—the perfect safe haven for a fugitive on the run.

Salva's words had made sense. Still, Kristen had insisted on seeing a doctor. The next day her husband had sent for a neurologist. Dr. Eden—George to her husband—had explained her condition, calling it retrograde amnesia. In Kristen's case, the blow to her head in the boating accident had been the culprit for her memory loss. In most cases the amnesia wasn't permanent, Dr. Eden had attested. There was, however, no medicine or treatment to reverse her condition.

Three years later, Kristen was still playing a waiting game, still unable to remember anything past the morning she'd opened her eyes and learned she was the wife of a perfect stranger. A very dangerous stranger.

"Then you forgive me, Princess?"

Kristen blinked out of her muse. "Forgive you?"

"For this morning."

She would never forgive him for *that* or for any of the other times he'd forced himself on her. But Kristen carefully nodded, her gaze drifting over the imposing naked body that lay beside her, knowing full well that whether she forgave him or not had nothing to do with the outcome of the next few hours.

In the moonlight, all six feet, two inches of Salvador Maland radiated danger and authority. He was the perfect male specimen—a tropical tan on an athletic body, and sinfully handsome. His commanding dark eyes almost too exotic for a man.

The island women thought him breathtaking. Kristen thought him frightening. The man behind the model's build and the sculptured perfection was the epitome of arrogance—second only to his violent temper, which he demonstrated daily by making the maids cry and the guards shake in their boots. More than once Kristen had found herself backed into a corner pleading for mercy for herself or Amanda. And there, standing over her, wearing a smug expression while she squirmed like a vulnerable fish on a deadly hook, was this stranger who called himself her husband.

"I forbid you to leave this room tonight." He raised his arm to rest his sleek, shaved head in the palm of his hand. ''Amanda has a competent nanny. She doesn't need you sitting up with her or walking the floor.''

Kristen had learned she was pregnant only a few short weeks after she'd opened her eyes and found herself on the island. As if dealing with an empty head and a strange husband wasn't enough, for the next several months she had endured severe morning sickness. Seven months later she'd given birth to a little blond angel Salva had insisted they name Amanda after his mother, the island's wealthy Creole grande dame, Miandera Maland.

In the beginning Kristen had wanted to believe Salva. She had wanted the island paradise to be her and Amanda's refuge, and she had wanted Salva to be their savior—the hero every woman dreams of marrying. But as time passed it became clear that Salva was as dangerous and unpredictable as the jaguars that prowled the wildlife preserve at Cockscomb. He was a ruthless man, and his island paradise Kristen's prison—a prison she ached to escape.

''Did you hear me? You will not leave my side tonight. Is that understood?''

''Salva, be reasonable. Amanda's a baby. These rules of yours—''

Like a snake striking on instinct, he wrapped his fingers around Kristen's neck. She fell silent, knowing what it would cost her if she challenged Salva's authority further.

Her quick submission brought a gleam of satisfaction to his confident dark eyes. Slowly he traced her small, fragile mouth with a blunt-tipped finger. ''Amanda will learn her lessons eventually.'' His smile broadened, his eyes turning carnal. ''And you, my lovely, have waited long enough to be rewarded for being so forgiving. Lie back, Princess.''

Dread swept over Kristen. ''Salva, I don't feel—''

His long fingers slid down her neck, squeezing and cutting off her protest, demanding that she flatten out on the bed. ''You're amazing,'' he praised. ''So fragile, and so remarkably perfect. From the moment I saw you, I knew I had to have you.''

Lavish compliments—this was the way it started—the prelude to several hours of enduring a woman's worst nightmare. Dread seized the moment and Kristen began to beg. ''Salva, please... I'm bruised and—''

''Shh. This morning I was angry,'' he reasoned. ''Tonight that's not the case. I don't enjoy hurting you, Princess.''

''But you do hurt me!'' She regretted the words the minute she said them. His gaze turned brittle, and Kristen could see his temper begin to slowly build like a determined island storm.

''Are you thinking of denying me, Princess?'' His eyes lit up, ready for the challenge.

She shook her head.

He leaned forward and brushed his lips over her mouth. His breath scalded her with the sickening scent of mint. ''Mother says you've cast a spell over me. It's true I'm unable to get enough of you. It's been three years and I still...'' He paused, his hard gaze studying her young face. ''Are you a witch then, capable of bringing me to my knees? Or simply the most perfect creature a man could ever envision owning? I ask you, witch or wife, Princess?''

''Wife,'' Kristen answered, motioning to the wine that sat on the nightstand. ''A dutiful wife.''

He seemed pleased with her answer and, too, that

she'd remembered the wine. He reached out and spread her long pale hair over the white satin pillowcase. "You're my beautiful princess," he mused out loud, then whispered, "and I'm your king."

"I'm no princess," Kristen refuted. *Just a wife with no memory,* she thought. *A trapped wife, desperately seeking answers.*

His cold hand covered her breast and squeezed, then slowly, possessively, he worked her nipple into a hard knot with his thumb. As he kissed her, his powerful gaze penetrated her soft brown eyes.

What was it? Kristen wondered. What was she reading in his eyes? Was it suspicion? Had she been careless earlier when she'd slipped into his private office? Had she failed to wipe clean her fingerprints when she'd taken the gun? Or was he simply testing her...again?

Kristen forced herself to snuggle against her husband's naked body. Anything to distract him, she thought—even this.

"I need to see you," he insisted, and quickly made a rag of the expensive nightgown.

Stripped in a heartbeat, Kristen squeezed her eyes shut. Her heart hammered against her chest and her breath caught in her throat. The desperate keening sound that escaped her lips was mistaken for passion and with a satisfied grunt, Salvador Maland lodged himself inside her. "Much better, Princess. Much better than this morning. Much..."

Kristen had been waiting, listening for her daughter's birdlike voice to call to her. The moment she heard it, she slid from the bed, retrieved her robe, and left Salva sprawled on his stomach in a deep sleep. In

Amanda's room, she dismissed the nanny. "I'll stay with her, Celia. You go back to bed."

The nanny's eyes widened, and Kristen knew why—Salva had given her strict instructions to stay with Amanda the entire night. "No, Mrs. Maland. No, no! I can't leave."

"It's all right. My husband will sleep through the night. I'm sure of it," Kristen said, recalling the two empty bottles that sat on the nightstand in their bedroom—a testimony to her husband's passion for expensive wine. She ushered the young girl into the hall. "Don't worry, Celia. I'll see to Amanda's fussing, and you," she leaned to whisper, "if you're not tired, should check on Captain Carmichael. He may be in need of a little distraction from his nightly guard duty." She smiled, then winked at the pretty nanny.

The young dark-haired girl blushed. "Thank you, Mrs. Maland. You are so generous and kind."

As soon as Kristen was left alone with her baby daughter, she lifted Amanda into her arms. "We need to hurry, sweetheart."

Within minutes Kristen had Amanda dressed and sitting in the middle of the bed. The child resembled her mother, from her pale blond hair to her petite bone structure and delicate mouth. She was a shy little girl, with sweet brown eyes. Her mommy's eyes.

Kristen went in search of the small black bag she'd stashed earlier in the far corner of the closet. From the bag, she pulled out a pair of jeans, a black T-shirt, and dark deck shoes. She dressed quickly, and while repacking the bag with necessities for Amanda, her fingers grazed hard steel.

Kristen hated guns, but the .22 derringer she'd hidden in the bag looked almost toylike in size, thus not so menacing. She'd actually chosen it because it was the smallest gun in Salva's private collection and the one that might go unnoticed the longest. Then, too, it hadn't looked all that complicated to load or shoot. No, she didn't intend to use it on anyone. But the gun would be good for intimidation's sake if necessary. No one needed to know she had never fired one before—that is, that she remembered.

Convinced she was doing the right thing, Kristen moved on to the next stage of her plan. With trembling hands, she forced herself to do the unthinkable—an act no mother would ever consider if she had a choice. She drugged her beloved Amanda with a small chip of one of her prescription sleeping pills.

Twenty minutes later Kristen shouldered the black bag, lifted her sleeping daughter into her arms, and slipped soundlessly down the grand hall of the Maland estate. She already knew where the guards would be and which escape route to take out of the house.

Praying Celia had lured Davis Carmichael away from his post at the front gate, she left the house. She had made friends with the guard dogs the first year on the island—her kindness rewarded this day by reaching the iron gate without alarming man or beast.

Unattended... Silently, Kristen thanked Celia for enticing Davis into one of the private gardens. Lifting her sleeping daughter's foot, she punched the sequence of numbers she'd written on the sole of Amanda's shoe into the electronic keypad. As the gate opened Kristen blinked back tears and hurried to the sailboat docked a quarter mile down the beach. She didn't question her knowledge of sailing as she boarded the sleek vessel and stowed Amanda safely below; she simply thanked God for gifting her with a means to escape.

Minutes later the boat moved away from the dock. A few minutes more and Kristen hoisted the white sails to catch the tropical breeze. A mile from shore, she pulled the photo from her pocket. It was one of six she'd stolen from a file in Salva's office. She didn't know the man in the picture, but her husband must—Salva had gone to a lot of trouble to have the picture blown up to cover one entire wall in his office.

In the moonlight she studied the reckless-looking man with the shaggy black hair. He appeared to be in his mid-twenties. His sun-baked muscular chest and massive biceps looked as if they'd been carved from a slab of iron. His long, oaklike legs were crammed into well-worn jeans, and his feet were bare.

He had the look of a fisherman.

The unexpected assumption simply popped into Kristen's head as she searched the photo. The background was out of focus, but the iron man was hunkered down over a hydraulic winch used on a fishing boat.

Hydraulic winch?

How did she know what he was repairing? Or that the winch was part of a fishing boat? Had she suddenly remembered something connected to her past?

From the moment Kristen had planned her escape, her destination had been St. Petersburg, Florida. It made sense. Salva said they'd met there.

But now…

She flipped over the photograph, anxious for another memory to pop out of thin air. On the back was written the name ''Blu Devil,'' and beneath that ''Algiers, Louisiana.'' Once again she brought her gaze back to the man in the photo, willing him to speak to her in some way.

Was it possible she knew him, possible he knew her? There had to be a reason why she'd been drawn to his picture besides his good looks.

Kristen had waited three years for a clue as to who she was. And now, suddenly, here it was. She could be trading one nightmare for another, but if there was a chance the Blu Devil was the answer to her prayers…the smallest chance.

Salvador Maland ground Davis Carmichael's face into the quarry stone beneath his feet while his mother, Miandera, watched. "You'll die slowly, Carmichael, screaming for a quick end. But it won't come. Kristen's gone and you say you don't know who invaded my home and abducted her. How can that be? You were the guard on duty."

"No more! Please, no more!"

Ignoring his plea, Davis was kicked in the ribs again where he lay on the terrace bleeding and moaning in pain. Close to becoming unhinged, Salva screamed, "No more, you say! There will be plenty more. She's gone, you bastard! Gone!"

Another vicious kick stole the guard's breath, the third rendered him unconscious. Salva motioned to the two guards who stood awaiting his instructions to take the man away.

"Yes, take him," Miandera insisted. "Then clean up this mess."

While the guards stepped forward to carry Davis Carmichael away, Miandera tangled her arm around her son and led him out of the gate toward the beach. Nearly as tall as Salva, Miandera Maland was sparrow-thin, and her sleek black hair was the longest on the island—reaching past her knees. Her skin was a golden brown from years spent in the Caribbean, her makeup as spare as her European smile.

As they walked the sandy beach, Salva admitted, "Kristen hasn't been off the island since I brought her here, Mother. She hasn't been out of my sight for more than an afternoon in three years. Dammit, how could something like this happen?"

"You feel betrayed. As you should, darling. The guards have failed you…us. They will be punished," she assured him. "And Kristen, if she left on her own, also must be punished."

Salva jerked to a stop and gazed down at his mother. "Are you suggesting that she's left me? That she snuck off in the night while I slept?"

"We must consider every possibility, darling. There was no forced entry. The dogs didn't even bark. And there's been no ransom request."

"Would that make you happy, to learn that she's betrayed me? You never liked her." Salva turned his hot anger on his mother. "Answer me! Are you happy that she's gone?"

"Nothing that pains you would make me happy, darling. And my granddaughter is also gone, remember?"

His mother had been jealous of Kristen from the moment she had laid eyes on her. But when Salva had told her about the baby that he and Kristen were expecting, Miandera had quickly tempered her animosity—a true Maland heir was rare, something to covet, to cherish and protect.

"I'm sorry, Mother."

"I have every confidence that you will return my granddaughter to me unharmed." Miandera reached for her son's hand and clasped it as they continued along the beach. "I did warn you, however, darling, not to fall in love with such a young girl. I do not say this to sting your pride, but Kristen never really came around as you had hoped—youth can be so fickle. She never understood the Maland way. And her lack of memory has been a problem from the beginning. She admitted once, she wished she could remember falling in love with you.''

Salva refused to react to his mother's criticism, or discuss Kristen's young age or lack of memory. ''Someone has breached the compound and taken them,'' he reasoned. ''I'm certain Kristen didn't leave on her own, Mother.''

''I hope you're right, darling. But the sailboat is gone. For what purpose would kidnappers steal the boat?''

''As a diversion, of course.''

''That's possible, yes.''

They walked on.

''I saw the bruises yesterday, darling. The ones on Kristen's arms. I only thought she may have left because—''

''She bruises easily, Mother.''

''I'm not criticizing you, darling. Some women need a strong hand. I suspect your young bride is one of those women.''

Salva refused to believe Kristen would leave over a few silly bruises. And yet, they had searched the entire island without gleaning a single clue.

''The yacht is ready,'' Miandera supplied in her husky voice. ''All Porter needs is a destination. Where will you search first?''

''I have a phone call to make, then I'll decide.'' Salva stopped and reached into his pocket for his cell phone. Seconds later he heard the voice of a man he had hoped never to talk to ever again.

"Crawford's Boat Tours."

Salva didn't identify himself. All he said was, "She's missing." It was a long shot, but he needed to ask anyway. "Have you seen her?"

"No. Don't tell me the bitch is on her way back here?"

"I don't have a confirmation on that just yet, but she is gone."

"Still empty-headed?"

"Yes."

Salva turned away from his mother's questioning gaze. He didn't want to think about what would happen if Kristen stopped taking her medication and started to remember. He only knew for all concerned, he had to get her back before that could happen. And he had to do it while keeping Miandera on a short leash. There were things he hadn't told her. Things his mother must never find out.

"What about your kid?"

"Gone, too," Salva answered.

"In your line of work it doesn't pay to have weaknesses, Maland. The bitch is your weakness. You should have had your fun with her, then killed her."

Salva didn't want to hear what he should have done. Three years ago he had simply taken what he had wanted and damned the consequences. It had always been the Maland way. His little *princess* had, indeed, become his weakness. But he wasn't prepared to give her up—not at any cost.

"She'd only come here if she started remembering. Let's hope *Little Krissy* stays stupid."

"You have my number. Day or night, call me if you

see her.'' Salva disconnected the phone and slipped it back into his pocket. Facing his mother, he said, ''Tell Porter we'll hold one more day. If I haven't received a ransom note, and Kristen still doesn't turn up on the island, I'll head for St. Petersburg.''

''And the Blu Devil? What of our plans for him?''

''We put them on hold for the time being.''

''On hold? But we've already done that too many times. You promised—''

''Be patient a little longer, Mother. A Maland's promise is his honor. I give you my word that the Blu Devil will die. But first, I will see that Kristen and Amanda are brought back to the island. And, if there is punishing to be done, I will see to that, too.''

Chapter 2

The dockside stench could curl a sensitive nose at twenty paces. The tourists who frequented the waterfront in Algiers, looking for a taste of culture, complained it griped their bellies and killed their appetites, too.

Blu duFray had grown up on the docks and, as a seasoned fisherman, he rarely noticed the ripe odor or the refuse and floating beer cans as he unloaded his day's shrimp catch off the *Demon's Eye*—his favorite among the fleet of seven aging shrimpers he owned.

Today's heat had crowned one hundred, a humid hundred that had forced Blu out of his T-shirt well before ten that morning. He wiped away the sweat clinging to his neck and glanced around, noting he and his crew were the last to unload their day's catch. By now the others were either on their way home or on a bar stool at Cruger's.

Out of the corner of his eye Blu saw something dark

move and he turned in time to see a nun perch herself on a crate outside Thompson's Fishery. She looked miserably uncomfortable as she fidgeted in the hot sun. She damn well should be, he thought, noting the way the black habit hid all but her small, round face.

He shook his head, sure she had been sent to sting his conscience and make him feel guilty. Well, it wasn't going to net her more than a heatstroke, Blu determined. Everyone knew the Blu Devil didn't own a conscience. And he sure as hell hadn't *reformed* like the hungry-for-a-story journalist at the *New Orleans Times-Picayune* had claimed. But whether he had or hadn't, the damage was done. Since he'd rescued those six kids from a slave trader last year, he'd been plagued weekly by mission-minded angels harassing him to donate a few extra crates of shrimp to their soup kitchens.

Frankly, Blu was fed up with the whole damn situation. Yes, he'd saved those kids, but there had been a reward, compensation for his trouble, and he hadn't been shy in accepting it. Still, his picture had been plastered on the front page of the newspaper along with a lengthy article playing him up as some kind of modern-day hero.

Well, the nun had made a trip to the docks for nothing unless she had a few extra pounds to sweat off, because his pockets were empty for whatever charity she was selling. No one on this side of the river except for Spoon Thompson—the wholesale crook Blu was forced to sell his shrimp to—could afford to ante up weekly for a tax write-off.

Blu glanced at the nun once more and found her

staring straight at him. Oh, hell, she was working him, all right. She had her eye on his shrimp.

Again, he cursed the unwanted publicity he'd received. If he had known how much trouble those kids were going to cost him, he would have never… No, that wasn't true; Taber Denoux had earned his iron cage, and those scared kids had deserved a happy ending.

He was all done questioning his actions. He may not like it, and most of the time he didn't, but long ago Blu had accepted that a higher power navigated his path. *Oui,* he was all through questioning why it had been him who had discovered Denoux's merchandise that night. In all honesty, he'd felt good seeing those kids reunited with their parents, but he'd also been eager to accept the sizable reward.

Yes, indeed, the Lord did work in mysterious ways—he didn't owe the bank his soul any longer, his men had regular pay checks, and he no longer had to work a second job.

An hour later, the shrimp unloaded and the boat cleaned, Mort said, "If that's it, you mind if I take off for a while? I got something to do."

"You got nothing to do, *mon ami,*" Blu drawled. "What you got is a few bucks in your back pocket and a memory burning your insides."

Mort grinned. "She had a pretty smile."

"I can't argue with that."

"If you were me, what would you do?"

Blu had no authority over Mort after hours. He'd been the oldest of the kidnapped kids Denoux had planned to peddle on the slave market—the only one who'd had nowhere to go after Taber Denoux had been put out of business and hauled off to jail.

It wasn't as if Blu had any regrets inviting Mort to join his crew. The kid had turned out to be a hard worker. He'd easily earned his wage, plus room and board. But from the beginning Blu had made it clear that Mort was expected to take care of himself. He didn't want the responsibility or the aggravation of keeping tabs on a teenager. He'd made it clear he didn't preach morals, give advances, or advice—hell, that would be like satan giving a lecture on the benefits of reading the Bible.

"You got something more for me to do?"

Blu shook his head. "No. Cross the river and take her someplace quiet."

Crossing the river meant catching the ferry and heading for New Orleans or taking the Crescent City Connection. The girl in question with the pretty smile worked at a hot dog stand along the Riverwalk.

"I'll see you later then," Mort promised.

"*Oui.* The *Nightwing* is all yours tonight. I'm staying at the Dump, again. I got payroll to finish," Blu explained.

The Dump—rather, the building in discussion—had been a purchase Blu made with some of the reward money he'd received for his "heroic deed." The rundown two-story on Pelican Street, a few blocks from where he'd grown up, seemed to be a good investment at the time.

He wasn't so sure of that now, though it had certainly pleased his mother and sister. They had been after him to *settle down*—preferably with a *nice girl.*

Blu had laughed out loud on hearing that, then promptly told them both that "settling down" was for old people, and that "nice girls" were for saints not devils.

He glanced in the direction he'd last seen the nun, but she was no longer there. Relieved the heat had driven her off, he pulled on his gray sleeveless T-shirt and jumped from the boat. Swearing as a burning pain shot into his left leg, he reached down to rub his thigh through his worn jeans as he headed toward the fishery.

The bullet wound, courtesy of the Denoux ordeal, had been slow to heal. The doctor had told him the infection he'd endured for the four days he'd kept the kids alive had resulted in permanent tissue damage and that he would always walk with a limp.

The minute Blu walked through Thompson's front door, Spoon looked up from his desk and grinned. He was a short, wiry little man with gray hair and insightful green eyes. In his fifties, twice married and single once more, Spoon had stepped into his father's shoes in much the same way Blu had; the only differences between the two men was their age and which side of the desk they worked on.

"A good catch today, duFray. You doubled my boys."

"Always do."

Blu's blunt reply didn't offend Spoon. The duFray Devils were top-notch, and no one in Algiers would argue that fact, or that Blu duFray was the number one reason why his fleet was still in business.

"Like I've always said, you got the nose for it. Your daddy had it, too. But I think yours is even better. They say you can't teach it. I sure as hell believe it. That's what makes your nose worth paying through the nose for.'' Spoon chuckled at his own joke.

Blu remained stone sober.

At twenty-five, he was the youngest fishing fleet owner in Algiers. But it wasn't Blu's age or ability that had sparked the number of outrageous wagers down at Cruger's Bar over the past few years—with his uncle Pike's help, Blu had taken over the duFray Devils at age eighteen after his father had unexpectedly died. No, the wagers had nothing to do with whether Blu was smart enough to step into his daddy's shoes, but whether the ''old tubs''—as his boats were referred to—would be able to stay afloat, what with the inflated prices on repairs over the years by the marine yards and the decreasing wholesale prices on shrimp.

''Name your price, duFray,'' Spoon insisted. ''Today I'm feeling generous.'' Blu opened his mouth, but the older man held up his hand. ''I've offered to buy you out before, I know. But I'll say it again, *mon ami,* you're too young to be workin' like you do and gettin' paid half of what you're worth. If I was you, I'd lighten the load and—''

''You're not me.''

''But if I was—''

''You got my tally ready?''

''I can appreciate you feelin' loyal to your daddy's memory, son. But if you would have taken my offer two years ago your reputation would still be worth a damn and your mama could hold her head up like she used to.''

"Leave it alone, Thompson, or I'll head over to Paradise Point and sell my catch to old man Aldwin."

"That'll be hard to do. Ain't you heard? He's all washed up. Under-sellin' me finally bellied him up. Either that, or that no-good worm of a grandson sucked him dry." Spoon grinned, obviously pleased with the other man's misfortune no matter what had caused it. "Besides, I heard you and Aldwin had a partin' of the ways a year or so ago. Don't suppose you'd care to set the record straight as to why that was?"

Blu had no intentions of trading information with Spoon Thompson. What had passed between him and Perch Aldwin was business of another kind. And it was too late to make amends—he'd already tried.

Spoon shook his head. "One of these days those old tubs of yours ain't gonna make it back in. Why don'tcha—"

"My tally," Blu reminded, growing tired of the sound of Spoon's voice and the same topic they argued over daily.

"Those old tubs are bleedin' you."

"Those 'old tubs' still top your catch any day of the week."

Spoon stood and came around the six-foot cypress desk. Side by side, the top of his egg-shaped head didn't reach Blu's massive shoulder. "It ain't the tubs, boy. Your nose is what's gettin' the job done. I've got the money and you've got the talent. Together we could go places. How about meetin' me at Cruger's in an hour and we'll settle this once and for all?"

"Save your money and your jaw, Thompson. I'm not interested."

"You're a stubborn bastard, boy. Ornery as hell, just like your daddy was. But one of these days you'll see I'm right." That said, Spoon picked up the tally sheet and handed it over. "I'm gonna keep askin'."

Blu eyed the tally, didn't like the figures, but knew it was the best he was going to get. He shoved the paper in his back pocket, then left without another word. Outside, he started up Bay Street, considering Spoon's offer, as he did at least once a week. He knew a number of independent fishermen who would jump at the chance to sell out to Spoon and go to work for him. And it would certainly lift a mountain of bills and worry from his shoulders if he did. But for thirty years the duFray Devils had been in business for themselves, and Blu couldn't get past the feeling that selling out to Spoon wouldn't only be selling out his father's legacy, but his men and their pride and dignity, as well.

A block from the waterfront, Blu realized he was being followed. He wasn't selling his fists to Patch Pollaro any longer, but the number of enemies he'd made working for the loanshark could easily explain the tail.

He picked up the pace and turned down Poke Alley—his limp always more pronounced at the end of a long day. He pulled the bandanna off his dark head and shoved it into his back pocket. His jeans were dirt-stained, his T-shirt a little better off since he'd worked most of the day shirtless. When he reached a deserted courtyard, he ducked inside. Minutes later, the tail crept past and Blu reached out and grabbed—his reputation for having the quickest hands in the fist business aiding him instinctively.

The scream that permeated the air jolted Blu's

senses. He'd been anticipating a man, but the scream was definitely feminine. He spun the figure around and promptly let go of the nun he'd seen hanging around the wharf an hour ago.

"What the hell are you after, church mouse?" Blu demanded, staring into a pair of wide eyes the color of brown sugar. To go along with her pretty eyes was a delicate nose and a rosebud mouth that was too sexy for the profession she'd chosen. She was, however, carrying the appropriate prop—a thick black Bible.

The nun quickly regained her bearings and took two giant steps backward. "I need to talk to you," she said in a hushed tone. "I'm interested in… What I wanted from you was…"

Blu groaned, anticipating her request. "Save it, church mouse. I'm fresh out of cash, and my day's catch has already been sold. You're hitting on the wrong sucker."

"I don't want your money, or your *catch,*" she responded. "And I'm sure I have the right sucker…uh, I mean, the right man."

"Don't you people get tired of holding out your hands like beggars?"

Disgusted, Blu curled his lip and pierced her with his well-known devil's stare—the one proven to make even the dockside roughnecks squirm—then turned away and started down the alley.

"Wait! Please, I—"

Dog-tired, his leg throbbing, Blu ignored her sudden pleading tone and kept walking.

"Hold it right there, Blu Devil."

Her pleading tone was gone. And the fact that she

called him by name alerted Blu that this wasn't the normal charity harassment he'd grown accustomed to—most of the nuns he'd faced were shy and could barely look him in the eye. They had also addressed him as Mr. duFray, even though his *devil* reputation preceded him.

He turned just as she flipped open the fat black Bible and pulled out a small .22 derringer. Aiming it straight at him, she said, "I need your undivided attention. Do I have it?"

Blu stared down the barrel of the palm-size handgun. "You've got it, church mouse. What's this about?"

"Not a handout," she assured. "Information will do fine."

"What kind of information?"

"How do you know Salvador Maland?"

The question wasn't going to get an answer; Blu had never heard the name before. "I don't know anyone named Salvador," he admitted.

"Liar." She stuck the neat little pearl-handled .22 farther out in front of her. "You have to know him. He knows you."

"Plenty of people know me, *fille,* that doesn't mean I know them." Blu studied the gun, the petite young girl, then the gun again. "Is that thing loaded?"

"It wouldn't do me much good if it wasn't. Does the name Kristen Harris mean anything to you?"

"No."

"Are you sure?"

"Does she know me, too?"

Her hand started to shake, confirming she wasn't as tough as she was trying to make him believe. Suddenly her shoulders slumped and she let go of the Bible. When it hit the ground it made a wood-splitting noise and it was then that Blu realized it wasn't a Bible at all. It was a wooden box meant to look like one.

The nun dug a picture out from the folds of her skirt. "This is you, right?"

Blu took a step forward.

She shook the gun at him. "Stay where you are!"

Blu stopped, squinted at the picture. He decided it was definitely him. He was putting a hydraulic winch back together. He'd gotten good at repairing engines, too. And it took hours to repair nets and busted rigging, but his jack-of-all-trades ability was why he was still in business. "I guess that's me," he told the nun.

"I doubt there's two of you," she offered. "Besides, your name is on the back. And Sister Marian confirmed it's you." Her gaze followed his tall, broad frame up then down. "You don't exactly blend into a crowd, and everyone I talked to knew right where to find you."

No surprise there, Blu thought. He'd lived in Algiers all of his life. For the past twenty-five years his parents had owned duFray Fish, the fresh-fish market on Front Street. Then there was his stint with Patch Pollaro as hired muscle, not to mention last year's "heroic deed" that had gained him an altogether new fan base. Hell, yes, people knew him for one reason or another.

"Now what?" Blu forced his attention away from her sexy mouth. "What's next? You going to shoot me?"

"Not unless you do something stupid." She slipped the photo back into her pocket. "Show me your left hand."

The request had Blu arching his heavy black brows. "My hand?"

"Do it!" She motioned with the gun to encourage him.

Blu raised his hand for her to inspect.

"Turn it over."

He rolled it palm-side up.

"Nothing," she whispered, and a little sigh of relief followed. Then she closed her eyes and lowered the gun.

Surprised, but never one to let that cloud his judgement, Blu jumped at the opportunity to disarm her. He surged forward, but his boots scraping over the brick courtyard gave away his intentions. She blinked open her eyes, shook off whatever had come over her and quickly raised the derringer. "Get back!"

"Take it easy." Blu raised his hands. "Put the damn gun down, church mouse, before you drill me without meaning to. That thing wasn't meant to be waved around like a flyswatter. They usually have a hair trigger."

"Then I suggest you tell me what you know about Salvador Maland, or you just might end up a dead fly and tomorrow's news."

"I already told you, I don't know anyone by that name."

"How can you not know someone who has a ten-by-twelve of you in his office?"

Blu shrugged. "Maybe he likes my face."

"I don't think you understand. I'm talking ten *feet* by twelve *feet.* Your face covers the entire wall in Salva's office."

That was the weirdest thing Blu had heard in a long time. So weird, in fact, he sifted the man's name through his memory bank once more. But it still didn't produce a familiar face. There was a chance he'd dealt with the man indirectly while working for Patch, but to chase down the name he would have to pay his old boss a visit.

"This picture of me, the one on this guy's wall, is it recent?"

"It's the same one I showed you." She eyed his shaggy black hair, which was a couple inches shorter, but still past his collar. "Please, this is very important."

"Can you refresh my memory?" Maybe it was the desperate look she was giving him that had made him ask. But more likely it was that damn mouth of hers—she had the sweetest little lips he'd ever seen. "How about telling me how this guy and I might have met?"

His innocent question upset her. She waved the gun at him again. "Refresh your memory? Ha! How can I do that when I can't even refresh my own? You're the one who's supposed to be filling in the blanks here, not me. I traveled all the way from…" She clamped her mouth shut, aware she was on the verge of revealing too much.

"From where?" Blu prompted.

She wiped at the corner of one of her big brown eyes. "Never mind where."

Blu realized she was fighting tears. "Listen, *fille*, maybe if you put the gun down we could talk this over."

"There's nothing to talk over if you don't know

Salva or...Kristen Harris.'' She swore softly. ''This has all been for nothing. How could I have been so stupid?''

''Put the gun down.''

Blu watched as she lowered the gun. Then, just as quickly, she raised it again. ''I put the gun down and then we both walk away, right?''

Blu's answer didn't come quick enough.

''That's what I thought. You're not going to let me walk away, are you? Another big man with a big ego. How could I be so lucky?''

''Put the gun down,'' Blu growled in a bigger voice than before.

Defiantly she gripped the gun in both hands and took aim at his head. ''I don't think so. I think you should strip, Blu Devil.''

''What?'' Blu was sure he hadn't heard her right.

''I said, take off your clothes.''

''A nun demanding I get naked? That's a first.''

''It's not for the reason you think. I'm not dying to get a look at...at Harvey, or whatever you've named it. That look you gave me a minute ago suggests I won't get a block before you come after me. So I'm taking your clothes for insurance.''

She was right about him going after her. No one pulled a gun on the Blu Devil, then walked without paying for the privilege.

''Start with your boots.''

''Or you'll shoot me?''

She smiled then, a sexy little smile that showed off pearly white teeth. ''At this close range, I think I can hit what I'm aiming at. Don't you?'' She took aim at

Harvey. "How much do you enjoy being a man, Blu Devil?"

Not as coolly as he would have liked, Blu said, "No complaints."

"Then I suggest you protect your assets by pulling off your boots." To prove she meant business, she tugged back the hammer.

"*Bon Dieu, fille.* You don't want to do this," Blu warned. "I never forget a wrong. Never."

"I believe you're a man who means what he says, but I don't have a choice. Your boots, Blu Devil."

Swearing, Blu leaned against the brick wall and removed his left boot. Next, he pulled the right one. But just as he was setting it down, he dropped to his knees and hurled the number twelve at the nun's outstretched arm. The gun discharged as it hit the concrete, the bullet ricocheting off the bricks in the narrow courtyard like a Ping-Pong ball. On instinct he drove forward, snagged the nun by her long black skirt and dragged her down.

It was all over within a few hairy seconds, or so Blu thought until the church mouse hefted the boot that lay within arm's reach and clouted him alongside the temple with enough force to cause him to see stars.

Chapter 3

"You say she was wearing nun's clothes, but you don't think she was a nun?"

Blu turned from the window in the New Orleans Police Department and gazed at Ryland Archard, one of the NOPD's most respected homicide detectives. "I don't think too many nuns pack heat, do you, Ry?"

"She had a gun?"

"A fancy little .22 derringer. A specialty piece with a pearl handle."

"A nun with a gut warmer. That's a first for me."

"For me, too."

Blu saw the amusement in his brother-in-law's eyes. He knew how ridiculous it all sounded. He also knew what a slim chance he had of finding the gutsy little *fille*. But he was determined to try. He'd wrestled with the idea the entire night. Those damn eyes and her dainty pink mouth had kept him awake; that, and the headache she'd given him by crashing his own damn boot into his skull.

True, he was curious as to why Salvador Maland had put his face on an entire wall in his office, but that wasn't the primary reason why he'd shown up in Ry's office first thing this morning. Something important was driving that *fille,* something powerful enough to make her dress up in nun's garb and pull a gun on him. She'd been scared to death, and still she'd stood her ground.

Blu wanted to know why.

"I want you to help me find her." There, he'd said it. He'd asked his brother-in-law for help.

"Did I hear right? You want *my* help?"

The smug look on Ry's face was followed by an open-faced grin. Blu swore crudely. "*Oui,* you heard me. I've already cleared it with Brodie. I'm taking time off work and he's agreed to do double duty until I get back."

Ry's grin faded. "You've never taken a day off in your life. Well, not willingly anyway. Speaking of time off, Margo and I are headed for Texas for two weeks. She wants to meet my parents and brother."

"When?"

"We leave tomorrow."

"Your timing stinks." Blu saw the way Ry's brow arched. "Okay, so I was expecting more than just a little help. I know this isn't your field of expertise, but I really need to find this girl."

"If it's that important, I'll get in touch with Jackson. He can follow it up on this end."

Jackson Ward was Ryland's rebel partner—the loose cannon of the outfit. A man who was on suspension more than he was on duty because he didn't go by the book on anything.

"So Jackson's working?" Blu asked. "Last time we talked he was on suspension."

"He was just reinstated yesterday."

"That won't last long."

"It never does," Ryland agreed. "But when he's working, he's the best there is."

"I thought you were the best. That's what the paper claims."

"And we know that every word the paper prints is gospel, right, *hero?*"

Reminded of the harassment he'd endured over the past year due to *freedom of the press* over his "heroic deed," Blu snorted.

"So Brodie's willing to wrangle with Spoon Thompson on your behalf for a few days? That should be worth a front-row seat."

Blu grimaced. "*Oui.* Those two are about as agreeable as two cottonmouths fighting over the same rat. No, Brodie's not too happy about me taking time off, but he's a good friend."

"He proved it last year," Ryland agreed. "Not too many men I know would have lived through the beating he took from Denoux's men to protect you and Margo. No, Brodie Hewitt is a good man. Though I would certainly like to know where he calls home. No one seems to know his story. A man who keeps himself a mystery is a man who usually has something to hide."

Blu remained silent. He knew Brodie's story, but he'd sworn to keep it to himself. When Brodie was ready to deal with his past, he'd head home. But until then, Blu would value Brodie's friendship and the big guy's loyalty to the duFray Devils.

"Do you think this girl has something to do with your pal, Patch? You made quite a few enemies when you were working for him. Maybe she wants revenge for some old, unsettled score."

"Then why didn't she just shoot me? She had plenty of time if that's what she wanted." Blu walked away from the window and the warmth of the morning sun and sat on the chair in front of Ry's desk. "She asked me if I knew a man named Salvador Maland. She seemed to think I should. And when I said I didn't, she called me a liar."

"You're sure you *don't* know him?"

"I don't think so. Does the name mean anything to you?"

"Not offhand."

"She had the damnedest eyes," Blu mused, still unable to forget their warm color, or her sexy little mouth.

"This is personal, then?"

"Hell, yes, it's personal. Damn personal when a *fille* you've never seen before points a gun at your nuts and threatens to blow them off."

Grinning, Ry said, "Sure would have made a helluva headline for the *Times-Picayune*."

Blu evil-eyed Ry. "The girl pulled a gun on me and you're making jokes."

"You make it sound like it was the first time you've ever looked down the barrel of a gun."

"It was with a young *fille* backing it. Claiming to be a nun, no less."

"Is that what's bothering you, that it was a woman?"

"You're not listening. She was little." Blu held up his hand. "About this big."

"So she's maybe five four, not a woman, and not a nun?"

Blu swore and was halfway out of his chair when Ry pulled a notepad from his drawer and said, "Not so fast. Give me some facts."

Blu eased back down onto the chair. "You mean, a description?"

"Yeah. What did she look like? What was the color of those damnedest eyes?"

"Brown. Soft brown."

"Hair?"

"Didn't see it."

"You said she's young?"

"Real young. Eighteen at the most, And she's..." He held up his hand again. "Five feet, four inches sounds right."

"Any identifying marks? A mole or birthmark?"

"Didn't see any."

Ry glanced up. "I thought you were going to give me a description."

"She was covered in black from head to toe. You've seen a nun, haven't you? They wear black...everywhere."

"Everywhere?"

Blu refused to let Ry get under his skin. "I'll let you know once I find her."

"So what we've got is a pair of *the damnedest* brown eyes, and she's *maybe* four inches over five feet. And she's wearing black...*everywhere.*"

Blu wished he had something more to offer. "Ah, her mouth..."

Ry was waiting with his pen poised. "Yeah?"

"Ah, she's got... She's got great teeth."

"Teeth?" Ry tossed the pen onto the desk. "Well, hell, that makes all the difference in the world. We'll see her coming, then."

"I'm out of here." Blu was on his way up once more.

"Sit down," Ry growled. "I need some coffee. You want some?"

"No." Blu watched his brother-in-law stand and head for the coffeepot in the corner. Ry was an inch shorter than Blu's six-three, and where Blu's eyes were a deep chocolate, almost black, Ry's were as blue as the morning sky. His sandy-brown hair was cropped close to his head, and the comfortable jeans and boots he refused to give up after making detective, fit the rugged Texan perfectly.

At thirty-four, Ry's status with the NOPD had steadily climbed. He was not only considered a fine homicide detective, but the next in line for a promotion. But more importantly was his claim to being the luckiest man alive since he'd married Blu's sister—a beautiful nightclub singer twelve years younger than him, who kept the Toucan Lounge in the French Quarter packed to full-house capacity three nights a week.

"She gave me another name, too," Blu drawled. "She asked if I knew a woman by the name of Kristen Harris."

"And do you?"

"No."

Ry returned to his chair with a cup of coffee. He jotted the name down beneath Salvador Maland's. "So how did you and our little nun part company? How did you disarm her? Did you get the gun? We could trace—"

"No gun." Blu confessed.

Ry eyed the cut and fresh bruise on Blu's forehead. "What's that from?"

Blu hadn't intended to go into the details of how she'd gotten away from him, but if he didn't... "She, uh, she told me to..."

"She told you to what?" Ry prompted.

"To strip," Blu confessed grudgingly.

Ry was in the process of taking a sip of his coffee. He promptly choked and messed his shirt. "Dammit." He eyed the brown stain spreading on his broad chest, then, still scowling, looked back at Blu. "And did you?"

"Did I what?"

"Strip?"

"I took my boots off." Blu rubbed his temple, remembering the way she'd smashed the heel into his head. "I toppled her before I lost my pants. But then she hit me over the head with my boot."

While Ry laughed, and patted dry the stain on his shirt, Blu climbed out of the chair, jammed his hand into his jeans' pocket and paced back to the window. "It wasn't that damn funny."

"Normally I'd agree if it had happened to someone else. But you've got to admit it's not every day a nun asks the Blu Devil to strip at gunpoint, then knocks him out. With his own boot, no less."

When Blu only grunted, Ry sobered—a little. "Okay, let me run these names through the computer and give Jackson a call. When he finds out something he'll be in touch."

Before Blu could agree, his sister opened the door and stuck her head inside. Surprise filled Margo's eyes when she saw who stood in her husband's office. "Blu? What are you doing here?" When she spied the cut on her brother's head, she gasped. "Oh, my God! What happened?"

Blu touched his temple. "It's not worth mentioning, so don't ask." He shot Ry a look that told him to keep his mouth shut. His sister was as protective as a mama bear over a newborn cub. If she thought Blu *needed her,* she would likely cancel her trip to Texas.

Margo frowned at him, then glanced at Ry. "Is he telling the truth or is he hiding something?"

When Ry hesitated, Margo faced Blu, her hands landing on her trim waist. Her dark eyes—a matched pair to her brother's—narrowed with suspicion. "All right, let's hear it. You promised me and Mama that you were done working for Patch Pollaro."

"I am," Blu insisted.

"Then what's this?" She gestured to the cut on his head. "And why are you here? I can count on one hand how many times you've willingly set foot in this office."

"Margo." It was Ry's voice that brought her up short. "You promised you would back off and give it a rest. Harping ain't pretty, baby."

"Harping? I don't harp. It's called, I'm-your-sister-and-I-have-a-right-to-be-concerned." In a visible huff, she planted her butt in the chair opposite her husband and crossed her long legs.

Blu gestured toward Ry. "I was hoping once you married him, Chili, he'd take up all your worrying time."

His pet nickname for his sister didn't soften her. "I have plenty of 'worrying time' for all of my family. But in your case—"

"Easy, baby," Ry warned.

Margo brushed her black hair off her shoulders, her

gaze locked on Blu as she talked to her husband. "I can't help it, Ry. He promised me he would take better care of himself after nearly getting killed last year. And as far as I can see, he doesn't look like he's keeping his promise. I'll just bet Patch Pollaro is behind this."

"I told you, I quit him. Go down to the Red Lizard and ask Patch if he's seen me lately. He'll tell you he hasn't laid eyes on me in a year. I'm officially retired. I'm no longer breaking arms or fingers at a hundred dollars a pop."

Blu watched his sister squeeze her eyes shut in disgust.

"Don't talk about it."

"You brought it up."

"Then let's drop it."

Blu was about to agree when his stomach growled.

"Don't tell me you haven't eaten yet today? A shrimper who goes hungry." Margo shook her head. "Honestly, Blu, it's not like food is hard to come by. You just throw the nets out and—"

Blu threw up his hands and looked to Ry for help. "Now she's attacking the way I eat. And this is the woman you chose to wake up next to for the rest of your life?"

"And they say men don't whine." Margo stood and gave Ry her full attention. "I guess I'm off to feed him. Do you want— What's that on your shirt, honey?"

"Coffee."

"Coffee? Ry, coffee stains. I just bought you that shirt. Last night it was butter. This morning it's coffee. Do you think I should make an eye appointment for you?"

Ry scowled at his wife. ''Because your old man's eyesight is failing?''

The mischief in Margo duFray ran deep. And, like her brother, if she chose to remain stone sober a crowbar couldn't make her crack a smile. ''It's not my fault you're cresting the hill, honey. If you need glasses—''

''I can still pick a lock, can't I?''

''Yes. Last night you actually—''

''This is sweet,'' Blu interjected, ''but could we—''

Margo rounded on her brother. ''How would you know anything about sweet? Who have you been practicing on lately?''

''No one. I don't date, remember?''

''No, but you should. There's this new waitress at the Toucan who—''

''Is very nice,'' Blu finished. ''Forget it.''

''What's wrong with nice?''

''Nothing.''

''So you never plan on bringing anyone to Sunday dinner? Never?''

''Never isn't a word I feel comfortable using, but it probably fits in this instance.''

Blu knew Margo's concern for him was genuine. She had sacrificed a great deal for him last year. She'd taken a bullet in her arm, a bullet that had been meant for him. She'd survived the ordeal, and now that she'd been reunited with the only man she'd ever loved, her current mission was to find her outlaw brother a *nice* wife.

Blu's stomach growled again.

''I heard that. Come on. While I'm feeding you, I'll tell you about Sharon.''

''Sharon?''

''The *nice* girl at the Toucan.''

As Margo passed through the door, Blu hung back. "Thanks for your time, Ry. Tell Jackson I'll be anxious to hear anything he finds out. Oh, and make sure you take care of my sister in Texas. She's hard to live with most days, but I wouldn't want to have to try living without her."

The devil's lair was a pigsty. Kristen crept inside the desecrated apartment, her eyes wide with disbelief. How could anyone live in such a depressing place, she thought, as she scaled the stairs and entered the apartment at the top of the landing.

The air smelled old and damp, and she wrinkled her nose, unconsciously wiped her hands on her jeans-clad thighs. There was no place to cook a meal, no chairs or table. Nothing but an old mattress lay in the far corner.

The bathroom—Kristen stuck her head inside a small archway and found a dingy yellowed sink, a toilet in worse condition, and a shower stall rimmed on all sides with rust. Suddenly she felt lucky that she had found the women's shelter on Carmel Avenue. She couldn't afford to stay in a motel, and an apartment such as this would have been no place for Amanda. The shelter was clean, and the food tasty and regular. And there was this wonderful nun named Sister Marian who had befriended them. That's who had lent her the black habit yesterday, and who had agreed to baby-sit Amanda today while she was out.

Kristen released a defeated sigh. Yesterday she had hoped that the Blu Devil would recognize her, and when he hadn't... Well, maybe he didn't know her, but he certainly knew Salva. That's why she was in his apartment—to find evidence he had lied. Evidence that might give her another clue as to who she was and where she belonged.

She had stared at his photo a number of times on the sailboat, then on the airplane. As wary as she was of the man and his possible connection to Salva, she'd started hoping he was her brother, or maybe a mean cousin who valued family. She'd imagined him seeing through her nun's disguise and telling her that he was thrilled she was alive and well. Then he'd call her by name and take her home to meet the rest of her family—all ten brothers who looked as tough and solid as he did.

Fairy-tale garbage, is what it all was. The Blu Devil couldn't possibly be related to her. Kristen glanced around the room and shuddered. No, she couldn't be related to anyone who lived like this.

Exhausted, she admitted her bravado was slipping. She was confused and afraid. She wanted to go home, but the only home she remembered was the one on the island and she didn't intend to go back there. Not ever.

Salva would be searching for her by now, and just thinking about how he would punish her if he ever found her made her sick to her stomach. He had contacts all over the country. Once he'd turned Belize upside down, she was sure he would dissect the coastal towns one by one.

She would have gone to the police if she hadn't been so afraid that Salva was telling the truth about her fugitive status. She didn't feel like a criminal, but she couldn't take the chance. Not with Amanda's future hanging in the balance.

But all was not lost. At least, not yet anyway. Yesterday when she'd asked to see the Blu Devil's hand and it was free of Salva's mark, she had actually felt momentarily dizzy with relief. The Blu Devil was not one of *them*—he didn't carry the Maland dagger insignia tattooed into the palm of his left hand. And if he wasn't one of *them,* then it was quite possible he was Salva's enemy. That would explain the picture—her husband was big on vendettas. Once he'd had a statue constructed in a man's likeness just so he could destroy it piece by piece over a week's time.

Kristen had watched the Blu Devil for three days before she'd approached him. What she'd learned wasn't anything concrete, but she had come to realize that, physically, he was an iron man. That his fleet of shrimpers docked full daily, and that he was always the last man to leave the wharf at the end of the day.

In the midst of her musing, Kristen heard footsteps on the stairs. Jerked back to the present, she sucked in her breath. Was it him? Had the Blu Devil come home? No, it couldn't be him. What would he be doing here at this time of day?

She glanced around, knowing there was no place to hide—she couldn't even crawl under the bed.

Filled with a sudden urgency, Kristen dashed for the door and flung it open. Bolting into the hall, she knew she had only a few seconds before whoever was climbing the stairs reached the landing. With no time to lose, she grabbed for the first doorknob she came to and nearly stumbled over her own feet to get inside. Heart pounding, she eased the door closed, hoping she hadn't made too much noise. Her gaze took in the room in one quick glance. The rundown apartment was no better than the one she'd just vacated. In fact, it was exactly the same—bare of furniture, with only a mattress in the corner.

She glanced at the wall that separated the two rooms

and to her horror realized that the shell of a wall was missing large pieces of plaster. In some places she could actually see into the next room through the narrow cracks. At that moment it occurred to her that maybe she'd been wrong, maybe this wasn't the Blu Devil's home, after all. But she'd followed him here yesterday after he'd pulled himself to his feet in the alley, and the day before that.

Oh, God, what if it had all been a trap? What if he had known she'd been following him? What if he'd gambled on her coming back?

Worse, what if it wasn't the Blu Devil at all? What if Salva had been on her trail from the moment she'd left the island?

Chapter 4

It was *him.* It was the Blu Devil.

Kristen covered her mouth as she peered through the crack in the wall, another dose of fear lodging in her throat. She squeezed her eyes shut and tried to think of a way out of the building without being seen. At the very least, heard.

As scared as she was, she felt an overwhelming amount of relief that it wasn't Salva.

It was strange to fear the Blu Devil and at the same time want him to be her savior. His wild hair was so black it looked almost blue, she thought, squinting through the crack. It appeared stubborn, too, as stubborn as his ruggedly built jaw. His good looks were understated by his fierce, dark eyes and serious, hard mouth. It gave the impression he had never smiled a day in his life. His broad shoulders were as intimidating as his long muscular legs and the size of his hands.

Kristen didn't like *big men,* didn't like their forceful

natures. She knew her fear was irrational; not every man enjoyed dominating a woman with force, but she had suffered so much at the hands of a *big man* over the past three years that she'd become jaded. And, she reminded herself, she'd seen this man in action—the Blu Devil wasn't just strong, he was as quick as a bolt of lightning. Not even his limp seemed to slow him down.

He peeled off his white sleeveless T-shirt in one complete motion and tossed it onto the mattress in the far corner. He was beautifully put together—bodywise there would be few men who could equal him. Even Salva didn't compare, Kristen decided as she examined every exposed muscle in the Blu Devil's broad back.

She continued to stare through the crack, determined to find something about this man that might spark her memory. But she found herself again distracted by the sight of him—afraid one minute, in awe the next.

He rolled his head side to side. Stretched. When he reached for the zipper on his jeans, Kristen sucked in her breath and held it. Suddenly his hands stilled. A second later, he lifted his head and slowly turned to stare at the wall she was hiding behind. The crack she was peering through was tiny. He couldn't possibly know she was there. Still, Kristen jerked her head back and flattened herself against the wall. Surely he hadn't sensed she was watching him, not unless he had the predatory instincts of a wild animal.

A long minute passed. Then another. More minutes came and went. Kristen took several calming breaths, and shook off her paranoia. Still, she needed to get out of there. It was going to be tricky, but she was going to have to try.

She was still debating her dilemma when something

hit the wall with such hellish force it literally bounced her into the middle of the room—something hellish, like an angry oversize fist.

Oh, God! Kristen let out a wild cry, then scrambled for the door. As she thrust it open, she came face-to-face with the Blu Devil. She screamed and slammed the door shut, at least she tried to—the door flew back open, nearly shearing off her nose. She turned to run, her gaze darting around for an alternate escape route. But she already knew there was none, not unless she dove out the second-story window.

She hadn't made it halfway back into the room before a powerful arm curled around her waist and hauled her off her feet. It happened so fast she was left peddling air.

The power that snaked around her and reeled her in was double that of Salva's. The realization that he was ten times stronger than her husband, sent total terror flooding through Kristen's veins. She'd suspected he was strong—but...my God!

She swung her arms and flayed her legs, relieved when a solid kick netted a grunt of displeasure. Encouraged, she remembered his limp and swung her fist in the direction she hoped his thigh would be. The second swing hit its mark. He swore crudely and loosened his hold on her for a split second. Kristen spun around and kicked in the direction of his groin. Anticipating her move, he jerked sideways.

A second later he charged her.

She shrieked as he drove her backward. Following her down, she ended up sprawled on the smelly mattress in the corner with the Blu Devil on top of her.

Momentarily dazed, Kristen blinked, then focused on a pair of fierce dark eyes studying her long and hard.

A minute passed then he said, "I think we've already had this dance, *fille. Oui,* now I remember." And to prove that he did, his hand reached up to touch the cut on his temple.

Blu could feel her frail yet shapely body beneath him—feel every inch of her. And whether he wanted it to or not, the perfection that had been hidden by the black robe yesterday put a new slant on everything; his little nun had enough curves to sober a career drunk.

A perfect package, he mused—beautiful eyes, a sexy mouth, angel hair and a killer body.

Killer?

"Where is it?" Blu demanded, quickly coming to his senses.

"Where's what?"

"The gun, dammit?"

"I didn't bring it with me."

"Sure you did." Blu shifted his weight and ran his hand over her left hip. He felt her body tense.

"Please," she pleaded, "don't hurt me."

Blu ignored her plea, reminded of how easy it had been for her to aim that .22 at him yesterday. Determined it wouldn't happen again, his hand kept moving as he watched her. Her eyes were wide, her fear stealing her air. "Breathe, dammit, or you're going to pass out," he warned. "If that happens, you'll wake up not knowing what I did to you."

His words made her cry out, and the air rushed back into her lungs.

"The gun," Blu insisted. "I want it."

"Please! I—"

Blu got to his knees and flipped her over so quickly she didn't have time to fight him. And that's when he saw the bruises covering the backs of her arms. He'd seen hundreds of bruises, in all shapes and sizes; had been responsible for more than he cared to remember. Good at his past job, he knew just how much pressure to inflict to cause a man's skin to discolor, and to what degree. There was no question about it, his little nun had been manhandled, and it had been fairly recent.

The small bulge in her back pocket caught his attention, and he shoved his hand inside and retrieved the derringer. Confident she would have better manners now that he had disarmed her, Blu shoved to his feet.

"Get up."

She rolled over, scrambled to her feet and took several steps back. With shaky hands, she shoved her sleeveless blue blouse back into the waistband of her jeans, then brushed the length of her hair away from her face.

Blu watched as her fairy-tale hair drifted over her shoulders, then past her arms, then past her waist. Hell, he'd never seen hair that long or that satin-smooth in his life.

Yesterday, dressed in nun's clothes, she'd pulled a gun on him and given him one huge headache. Today, dressed in street clothes, he'd caught her spying on him like a little pervert. What the hell was she after?

Blu waved the gun at her. "So we've established you're not a nun. And you like skin."

"Skin?"

"Yesterday you were ordering me to get naked." Blu motioned to the wall. "Now I catch you copping a peek through a crack in my wall."

Her cheeks heated. "You have it all wrong."

"Then set it right."

"I told you yesterday why I wanted your jeans. You

couldn't answer my questions, and I couldn't trust you to just let me walk away. Today I wasn't watching you. Well, I was, but I didn't come here to do that. You were supposed to be at work."

"And?"

"And I thought you were lying about knowing Salva. I came to see if I could find some proof." She paused. "But when I got to your house—"

"This isn't where I live. It's just a place I own."

"Oh..."

Blu gauged her expression. She looked genuinely surprised. "I told you the truth yesterday. I don't know your friend. I've never heard of the Harris woman, either."

"You have to know Salva."

"What I know is, you're beginning to annoy me." Blu aimed the gun at her. "And just so you know how it feels to be on the receiving end, get naked."

"What?"

"You heard me. Forget the shoes. Start with the blouse."

Her big brown eyes turned huge. She shook her head. "Yesterday I was desperate," she pleaded.

"Desperation has its price," Blu countered. "Let's see some skin."

"No!"

Five feet, four and a half, Blu decided. She was a half inch taller than he'd told Ry. But he was right about her being young. Suddenly his curiosity made him ask, "How old are you?"

She jutted her chin. "Twenty-four."

Blu pulled back the hammer as she'd done to him yesterday. "Let's try that again. How old are you?"

"If you don't like twenty-four, pick your own number."

What he liked was her spunk. Hell, the whole package was a five-star winner. Her legs were slight, her breasts small but clearly visible. And all that damn hair was making him think of fairy princesses and peach-scented skin.

"My money's on eighteen," Blu offered. "Okay, Angel, come clean. Why are you stalking me?"

"I told you why already. I'm looking for information on Salvador Maland. Because you know him, I thought you would share what you know. Since you weren't willing to cooperate yesterday, and you're usually at work this time of day, I came to see what I could find out on my own."

That she knew his schedule meant she'd been spying on him long enough to know his pattern. Why? Was she telling him the truth? He saw her glance at the open door, then back at him. He shook his head. "You won't make it. Even with this limp, I'll catch you."

"Maybe not."

Blu was staring at her mouth, recycling Maland's name through his memory bank another time when she decided to bolt. Swearing, he raced after her, determined to stop her before she made it out the door. Too late, she was in the hall racing for the stairs before he knew it. Her hair was flying behind her like a wild mane, and he reached out to snare a hunk. Netting nothing but air, he swore again, then watched her leap onto the banister sidesaddle and slide to the bottom. Shocked, Blu roared out his protest, knowing that he'd seen the last of her.

She swung open the door and started through it. A moment later she darted back inside, slamming the door shut behind her. When she turned to face him, her cheeks were chalk-white and her brown eyes had grown to the size of silver dollars. "Please," she pleaded, "you've got to hide me. Please, you can't let him take me!"

She started to shake. Then she wrapped her arms around herself in an attempt to control her growing panic—at least that's what it looked like to Blu. Her eyes pleaded with him for understanding, but that was the problem; he didn't understand. But he damn well would, he vowed, as soon as he got rid of whoever was at the door.

He headed down the stairs and brushed past her to peer out the narrow window that aligned the door. Seeing Jackson Ward strolling up the sidewalk, Blu pulled back, shoved the derringer into his waistband, and reached for the doorknob.

"Please." She gripped his arm. "He might be looking for me. Please don't open that door."

Her words painted a little clearer picture, but not nearly enough. He said, "Jackson's a detective at the NOPD. He's here to see me, not you."

"The police!"

Instead of setting her mind at ease, she looked as if she was about to faint. "Oh, God! Oh-hh...!"

Blu glanced down to where her small hand clutched his forearm. Her tiny fingers were so small, her wrist as fragile as a twig.

The knock on the door gave her a jolt and she nearly jumped into his arms.

"I'll do anything." She was almost in tears. "Please, I promise. Just don't mention me to him. Please!"

Blu reached out, wrapped his arm around her waist and hauled her up against him. "I'm not sure what's going on, Angel, but until I get some answers, I don't plan on sharing you with Jackson or anybody else. So as soon as I get rid of him, you better be prepared to carry through on that promise you just made." That said, and ignoring how tense her body was in his arms, Blu lifted her off her feet and tucked her beneath the stairs. "Don't move. Not an inch."

In the middle of the second knock, Blu opened the door and faced Jackson Ward. "You look like hell."

"So does this place," Jackson answered back. "Still haven't started to fix it up yet, I see."

"No. But my excuse is money. What's yours?"

Jackson flicked his cigarette to the step, then ground it beneath his shoe. "The chief just told me Ry is six months away from a promotion. If he takes the desk job, I'll be looking for a new partner."

Ry had been the only partner Jackson had been able to keep in the three years he'd worked for the NOPD. It wouldn't be easy to find another, maybe impossible. Blu was sympathetic, and still had his head on another matter. He looked out the door and saw Jackson's aging green pickup sitting on the street. He checked to make sure no one else was hanging around, then took a step back to let his brother-in-law's partner inside.

Jackson stepped through the door and glanced around the old foyer. "This place looks like the last gang hideout I busted."

Blu eyed the peeling wallpaper climbing the wall along the stairway. "She looks tough," he agreed. "But she's solid brick on the outside, worth the investment once I fix her up."

The two men stood side by side. Both tall and dark,

they could have easily been mistaken for brothers, except for the fact that Jackson had cat-green eyes and a Chicago accent. But they were perfectly matched at six feet, three inches, both quick thinkers with rebellious natures, and enough nerve and grit to carry through on anything they felt was worth the trouble.

"So you're serious about moving in here?"

"Eventually. Margo says I've been portable long enough."

Jackson leaned against the door jamb and shoved his hand into the back pocket of his jeans. "A permanent home wouldn't be so bad if you had someone to share it with."

"Still looking for a wife?" Blu chuckled.

"Or a dog," Jackson joked, "that might be easier to live with. I talked to Ry after you left the precinct this morning. Ran those names for you."

"And?"

"And nothing. Want me to keep digging?"

It was clear his little nun was on the run—the look on her face when Blu had mentioned Jackson was a cop had confirmed that much. Questioning his next move, he gestured to the cut on his temple. "I woke up with a headache this morning. Before I cooled down, I went to see Ry. The more I think about it, the *fille* must have mistaken me for someone else."

"You think?"

"Yeah, I think. No sense you wasting your time on a dead end."

Blu opened the door and followed Jackson outside. Over the hood of the pickup, Jackson hollered, "Let me know when you want to start cleaning this place up. I'll give you a hand. I used to work construction for a few years back in Chicago before I turned stupid and decided to be a cop.''

Once Jackson had driven off, Blu headed back inside. He'd barely gotten the door closed when he came face-to-face with his little nun. ''You went to the police about me? Why?''

''Why? You pulled a gun on me yesterday,'' Blu pointed out. ''Damn near put my boot through my skull. My brother-in-law's a cop. I asked him to run those two names you gave me through the computer to see what he could find out. But as I'm sure you heard, they weren't able to get anything on either name.''

''Why didn't you turn me in? As you said, I pulled a gun on you yesterday.''

''Want me to call Jackson back?''

''No!''

''Then start talking,'' Blu demanded, leaning against the wall and blocking the only exit available to her. ''I think being up all night with a headache entitles me to an explanation.''

''I'm sorry,'' she repented. ''I—I'm Kristen Harris... That is, I think I'm Kristen Harris.''

''You think?'' Blu frowned. ''What the hell does that mean?''

She jutted her chin out stubbornly. ''It means that I *think* it's my name, but I'm not sure. I've lost track of some time.''

''Just how much time are we talking?''

Blu watched as she sat down on the stairs. She ran her hands through her endless hair, then settled them in her lap. ''Everything up until three years ago. I'd like to go home, but...'' She looked up, her brown eyes searching his face. ''I was hoping you could tell me where that might be. Only it looks like that's not going to happen."

"Why me?"

"I found the photo, and I— This is going to sound weird, but I knew just by looking at you that you were a fisherman." She paused. "And...and I knew it was a hydraulic winch."

"What?"

"In the picture you're repairing a hydraulic winch. I don't know how I know that, I just do. I thought it could be a clue to who I was."

She was right—it sounded crazy to know something but not why or how she knew it. But there might be something to it. A hydraulic winch wasn't the kind of thing a woman would pay much attention to. "You think you belong here? Belong here with...me?"

The question caused her cheeks to turn pink. She lowered her head again and stared at her hands. "You don't recognize me. No, I no longer think you and I have a connection, but I still think there is a strong possibility that you know Salva, even though you say no. Why else would he have your picture on his wall?" She sighed again, then stood. Brushing her hair away from her small face, she locked gazes with him once more. "I'm sorry for cracking you in the head yesterday, and for causing you more trouble today. I just wanted a clue so badly that I— Well, I'm sorry."

When she started past him, Blu reached out and locked his hand around her tiny wrist. "Not so fast."

"What now? I said I'm sorry. What more can I say?"

Blu jerked her arm up in the air. "You can explain these."

Her face paled and she tried to pull away. "Let go."

"These bruises are recent," Blu insisted. "Don't pretend you don't remember who gave them to you or why. Is Salvador Maland your boyfriend? Did he rough you up? Are you on the run? Will he follow, or is he already close behind? Is he dangerous, or just a jealous hothead?"

"Stop it!" Suddenly she wedged her hand between them and pulled the derringer from Blu's waistband. Jabbing it into his belly, she said, "Back off. I've had enough of big men thinking they have the right to manhandle me."

Blu released her, but he didn't move back. "Now what, Angel?"

"He's not my boyfriend. He's..." Her hand started to shake. "Please, just turn your back for a second. I'll be gone and I won't come back. I promise."

Blu didn't doubt the minute he did what she asked, she'd slip through the door and he'd never see her again. That fact didn't sit well, and because it didn't, with lightning speed, he knocked the gun from her hand and sent it spinning across the floor. A second later she was in his arms, pressed so close to him that he could feel her heart trying to jump out of her chest.

She started to fight him. When that didn't work, she began to cry. "Why couldn't you just let me go? I would never have come back. I—"

Blu set her away from him, shook her a little. Knees bent, he looked straight into her eyes. "It sounds like instinct brought you here. Well, dammit, let instinct keep you here. You'll never learn who you are or where you come from if you give up before you get started."

When he released her, she took a giant step back. "But you said you don't know Salva or..." Suddenly she backhanded the tears from her cheeks. "You know something, don't you? Please, if—"

"No, I don't. But I can nose around and see if I can find out who might." Blu waited for her to agree, hoping he wouldn't have to throw her over his shoulder and lock her up to keep her with him. But if she didn't see reason, he was prepared to do just that—though he didn't plan on analyzing why keeping her close had suddenly become so important to him.

"And what do you get out of this?" she asked.

Blu retrieved the gun from the floor, emptied it, then buried it in his pocket. Facing her once more, he said, "I get to find out why a man I don't know likes me so much he wants to look at me every day." When she didn't say anything, he added, "What do you say I grab a T-shirt and we take a boat ride? We'll clear our heads and see if we can figure out where we go from here."

Chapter 5

She didn't know he owned the *Nightwing*. The curious look she'd given Blu after he'd led her aboard the cruiser said it all. If she'd been spying on him—and she'd all but admitted she had—it was clear she hadn't been at it too long.

A year ago the *Nightwing* had gotten as much publicity as Blu had after the cruiser had successfully run down Taber Denoux's yacht as he and his cohorts had tried to escape New Orleans with Margo as hostage.

Yes, the sleek cruiser had been part of the heroic team that night, and she'd gotten her picture in the paper alongside Blu's. Naturally, the news media had jumped on the story of a poor fisherman's son who had scrimped and saved to own the boat of his dreams—the boat that had ultimately saved his sister from her evil kidnapper. It had made great copy and elevated Blu's unwanted hero status another notch. But the story was a fabrication of the truth. The real story was that

Blu's selfish need to own the *Nightwing* had overextended him financially. His father's fleet had been nearly lost until he paid Patch Pollaro a visit and had become the loanshark's hired muscle.

Blu steered the *Nightwing* away from the dock. Angel hadn't spoken since they'd left the apartment building, and he hadn't said much, either.

"I could change my mind."

Blu had just started the engine. He glanced over his shoulder to find her standing close to the railing, gauging the distance to the pier. "Meaning?"

"I could jump right now. I'm a good swimmer."

"So am I," Blu promised.

Her chin rose. "When you asked me on this boat ride, you made it sound like I had a choice. I really didn't, did I?"

"Sure you did. You had the choice of walking or being carried." That said, he settled behind the wheel, pulled back on the throttle, and the high-powered engine sent them forward. In a matter of minutes they were through the Outlet Canal, heading for open water. When she joined him at the helm, Blu glanced right to see her standing beside him as seaworthy as any seasoned fisherman. Her head was tilted to catch the day's warm air, her long blond hair lifting in the warm breeze. She looked like a ship's figurehead poised there—a desperate, beautiful maiden in search of her identity.

Mesmerized, Blu found it hard to keep from staring. He hadn't planned to take her very far, just far enough to give them both a chance to clear their heads. But the tranquil look on her face changed his mind and he followed the coastline south.

The next time he glanced at her, she had closed her

eyes and the rise and fall of her chest had slowed. She no longer looked scared and ready to bolt, but relaxed for the first time since he'd laid eyes on her. It was the water, Blu decided, that had calmed her, and it made sense. He'd grown up on the water, and though he should be used to it, if not bored by the sameness, he never dismissed the power it had to soothe him.

An hour passed before Blu finally cut the engine and set them adrift. Something had changed between them since they'd left the Dump. They were no longer adversaries, but it was too soon to call them allies.

Facing her, Blu said, "Feel better?"

She had stepped to the rail again, and after a long minute she turned to face him. She'd wrapped her arms around herself, but she couldn't be cold—there was no wind to speak of, and the tropical heat was over eighty degrees. "I can't explain it, but the water relaxes me," she confessed. "I've noticed it before, but I don't know why."

"Since I was a kid, I couldn't get enough of the water," Blu admitted. "Ma says I was born with salt water running through my veins."

"You have a mother?"

He was about to say, "Doesn't everybody?" but she'd said she didn't know who she was. That meant her parents were as much a mystery to her as her own name. "She runs the fish market on Front Street," Blu told her. "Has for thirty years. Her name's Rose. My father, Carl, died seven years ago."

"How old were you when he died?"

"I was eighteen."

"I don't think you realize how awful it is not to be able to put names to the people who are responsible for giving you life." She tapped herself on the head.

"Three years ago I woke up without a single childhood memory, and none of it has come back to me. Not any of it."

"Have you seen a doctor?"

"Yes."

"And?"

"And he couldn't promise that I would ever remember."

"But he didn't say you wouldn't?"

"No, he never said I wouldn't."

Blu came to his feet. "Maybe you should see another doctor. I'm not much on going myself, but—"

"No. I don't want to see another doctor."

For a long time the only sound that could be heard was the lapping of the water against the side of the *Nightwing*. Blu finally asked, "Do you know how it happened, Angel? How you lost your memory?"

"Yes. Salva said it was during a boating accident. Why do you keep calling me 'Angel'? I told you, I think my name's Kristen."

"Between yesterday's nun outfit, and—" Blu motioned to her waist-length hair "—I'll stick with 'Angel.' It suits you."

"Like Blu Devil suits you?"

"The name was my father's before it was mine—the devil part, that is. But I've been told it fits me better than it ever did him."

"Sister Marian said that—"

"Sister Marian? That's twice you've mentioned her. Is that whose nun outfit you were wearing yesterday?"

"Yes."

Blu moved to the stern where a leather bench wrapped the back of the boat. He patted the seat beside him, then watched as Angel cautiously curled up on the bench a safe distance out of his reach.

"Tell me about the past three years," Blu encouraged. "Then I'll..." Then he'd what? Get involved as he had last year? What was he turning into, the Red Cross? "Jackson, the detective that was at my place might—"

"I can't go to the police."

"Why? You shoot someone?" He'd meant it as a joke, but when her face paled, Blu kicked himself for being an idiot.

"I didn't shoot anyone. At least not in the past three years." She jumped up and headed for the railing. "I wouldn't have shot you in the alley yesterday. I hate guns."

Blu stood. She looked over her shoulder, saw him advancing, then glanced over the side of the boat as if she were contemplating jumping. On instinct, he reached out and snared her around the waist and hauled her back against him. "That would be suicide," he growled in her ear.

She tried to wiggle free, her backside making contact with his groin more than once as she fought. Blu tightened his hold on her and waited until the fight went out of her. Waited and suffered both at the same time.

When she finally gave up, she panted, "Suicide is getting the police involved before I know who I am. Please let me go!"

Her obvious fear of him was beginning to annoy him. Blu spun her around and cemented her to him so that he could see her face. "I didn't give you those bruises, so stop acting like I'm the scum who did. I haven't given you one damn reason to be afraid of me, have I?"

"You don't understand," she cried. "Salva's big like you, and he likes to...he likes—" She broke off.

Blu released her and backed off quickly. "Do I look like him?"

"No."

"Do I talk like him?"

"No."

"Smell like him? Dress like him?" His voice had turned angry.

"No!"

Blu had never questioned his ability to intimidate, other than to consider it an asset when he'd worked for Patch. Within a matter of weeks the rumor that came from the Quarter was that the Crescent City had its own home-grown devil, just like they had their own voodoo queen in Marie Laveau.

Only now, suddenly, that foreboding side to his character was getting in Blu's way, and he didn't know what to do about it.

"Take it easy," he heard himself say in a soft voice he hardly recognized. "I don't have a reason to hurt you. Most men don't get a charge out of manhandling women. There are a few, but I'm not one of them. I've never hit a woman in my life," he heard himself say. *But I've beaten the hell out of a hundred-plus men,* he thought.

"You're just so big. And—"

"Trying to swim for shore would be crazy. The deal is, I'll keep my distance so long as you keep your head."

When she continued to cling to the railing, Blu still wasn't so sure she didn't intend to jump. But if she did, he'd go in after her. Like it or not, it looked as though he was once again in the salvage business—the human salvage business, that is. Last year six dirty-faced kids had gotten under his skin, and now, in less than twenty-four hours, a frightened *fille* with fairy-tale hair had penetrated his thick skin.

Maybe the rumor that had been circulating since he'd left Patch Pollaro's employment was the truth. Maybe he had lost his edge and grown soft.

"I wasn't going to jump."

Her comment jarred Blu out of his musing. He studied her. She was so damn small standing there in her skinny little jeans. Her arms and hands were frail, and those big brown eyes... They just wouldn't let him go. *Oui,* the rumors were right—he was losing it—the Enforcer was dead, replaced by some idiot who, pretty soon, would be growing a damn conscience if he wasn't careful.

She looked away, unable to hold his gaze. "You keep staring. I wish you wouldn't."

"You can't be twenty-four," Blu stated. "Hell, you can't be twenty."

"Salva told me I was twenty-four."

"He's a liar," Blu said flatly, hating the man already and he hadn't even met him yet.

"You're still staring."

"The deal is, I get to stare and you get to be...cautious or afraid, or whatever it is you are of me. Maybe, after a while, we'll get used to each other's little quirks. Deal?" When she didn't say anything, Blu added, "There isn't anything you can tell me that would surprise me." When she still said nothing, he tried once more. "I can help you. I know that's a bold statement to make, and for now I don't plan on getting into why I can make that guarantee. You're just going to have to believe in those instincts of yours and put yourself in the hands of the devil. Think you can do that, Angel?''

Kristen turned to look at Blu for the first time since she'd taken his advice and confessed her desperate situation. It had been a long five minutes since she'd finished telling him her story, at least a portion of the story—she'd left out the part about being the *mother* of a two-and-a-half-year-old and the *wife* of Salvador Maland. She also hadn't mentioned the island that had been her prison for the past three years. But she had painted a picture—young girl awakens in a beautiful house with a stranger who says they are a couple. The stranger is rich and possessive. Powerful and abusive when angered. And since she can't remember anything, she stays.

Endures.

It was for self-preservation's sake, she told herself, that she hadn't mentioned being a mother or wife. Knowing the Blu Devil less than twenty-four hours, how could he expect her to bare her entire soul?

We'll have to accept each other's little quirks. And what if one of his ''quirks'' was steering clear of married women? Or, what if he hated kids? No, she'd been right to choose her words carefully.

He'd been quiet throughout her confession, and she continued to worry about that. Maybe he was going to change his mind, after all. Maybe he'd decided that helping her was a mistake.

''You said nothing would surprise you,'' Kristen reminded him.

He was standing at the back of the cruiser, a knee bent, resting it on the leather that wrapped the stern. It was his injured leg, the one that caused him to limp.

Suddenly he slid his leg off the seat and faced her. "You don't look like the type who would put up with a man who enjoys beating up women. What aren't you telling me, Angel? What are you hiding?"

"I'm not hiding anything."

"Maland have a reason to beat you?"

"No!"

Kristen would never confess the extent of her humiliation. It made her sick remembering the way Salva enjoyed torturing her, the way he liked to hold her down and watch the fear grow in her eyes before he hurt her. But all of it, all the abuse and degradation, was *her* pain to keep inside or to share, and she chose to keep it, to bury it deep and never let her shame out. The Blu Devil wasn't going to hear any of the sordid details because, frankly, she didn't want to see the disgust in his eyes, or the pity.

"Why did you stay with him so long?"

Kristen went for an easy lie. "Because he was rich and life there was easy."

"It isn't easy living with bruises. Try again."

"You don't know me."

"I know *big men* make you uncomfortable as hell. That says it all."

Kristen lowered her eyes. "All right. I couldn't leave."

"But you did leave. You're here. Why not a year ago, two years ago?"

"I don't know." Kristen couldn't keep the anger from seeping into her voice. Still, she refused to detail her reasons for staying. Amanda was so tiny, so vulnerable in the beginning; she had weighed less than five pounds at birth.

She watched as he turned back to stare out over the

water. The sun was setting and clouds were moving in. Dark clouds. The afternoon had slipped away and it was getting late. She needed to get back to the shelter, back to Amanda.

"Tell me more about the picture you showed me yesterday. You said you found it in a file."

"Yes. I found it in a file labeled Old Business."

"Was there anything else in the file?"

"No, just photos."

"Of people other than me?"

"Yes."

"But you didn't take any of the other pictures? Just the one of me?"

"I took six pictures from Salva's office, two of you and four of me." That wasn't entirely true, but Kristen wasn't going to mention Amanda's baby album that she had taken from Miandera's sitting room. "I didn't feel strongly about any of the others, so—"

He turned around, locked eyes with her. "Explain that."

He was looking at her in that hard, demanding way again. As uncomfortable as that made her, Kristen tossed her hair away from her face and met his demand with a bit of reckless defiance that was purely bluff. "I didn't connect with anyone in the other photos, all right? I didn't feel… I didn't feel something for any of the others."

"But the picture of me was different?"

Kristen felt her cheeks heat up. "Yes."

"Because you thought you and I— You thought I would recognize you yesterday. Isn't that right?"

He was suddenly looking at her with new eyes. Damn him for making her feel more vulnerable than she already did. "I told you why. I told you about the winch."

"But there was more, wasn't there?"

Yes, there was more. But she wasn't going to mention how, when she'd first seen his picture on the wall in Salva's office, she'd frozen on the spot for several minutes to stare at him. Her stomach…it had done an entire flip. Her cheeks were burning up now. "Okay, yes, I thought it was possible we were related. Then I thought you might work with Salva. But you don't have the tattoo so—"

"Hold it. What tattoo?"

"All the men who work for Salva have a dagger tattoo on the palm of their left hand."

He stood there for a long time considering her words. Finally he said, "I don't work for anyone but myself. And I've never seen you before yesterday. For sure, we're not related."

Feeling foolish, Kristen lowered her gaze. "I could show you the other photos. Maybe—"

"Do you have them with you?"

"No."

"Where are you staying?"

She looked up to find him staring again, only this time he was sizing up her figure, his fierce gaze locking on her breasts. She wanted to cross her arms over her chest, but instead she turned away and feigned interest in the sunset.

"I asked you, where are you staying?"

The words were so close that Kristen knew he now stood directly behind her. A gentle breeze lifted her hair and she angled her face to cool her cheeks and calm her racing heart.

"Come on, Angel. It's time you trusted somebody."

She shook her head. ''I could meet you tomorrow.''

''What makes you think I'm letting you off this boat tonight?''

Kristen spun around and found herself practically in his arms. ''Now you sound like Salva. You said you weren't like him. Please, don't be *him* now.'' When he didn't answer, she said, ''I don't trust anyone, and for now that's the way it has to be. That's the secret to survival.''

They were toe-to-toe. Kristen suddenly felt his fingers on the backs of her arms. Slowly he brushed them over the bruises. It was a shock, him touching her—no, not the touch, but the manner in which he was touching her—so gentle it was almost nonexistent.

Still caught up in his feather-light caress, she didn't move when he leaned forward. Bending his knees so he could move closer, he whispered next to her ear, ''The secret to survival, Angel, isn't a matter of not trusting anyone, but trusting the right someone. In this case, that would be me.''

The feel of his warm breath against her skin made Kristen shiver. His fingers were still moving over her arms, doing the oddest thing to her pulse. And her stomach was suddenly tied in dozens of tiny knots. He dropped his hands and took a step back. With nothing to say, Kristen simply stood there, drinking in the wild scent of the Blu Devil and scrambling to make sense out of what had just happened.

''We'll meet tomorrow night at Cruger's,'' he said, breaking the silence and the spell he'd cast over her. ''Nine o'clock sharp. Bring the pictures.''

Was he saying what she thought he was saying? Was he going to let her go?

Kristen had her answer an hour later when the Blu

Devil moored the *Nightwing* to DuBay Pier and helped her off the boat. "Tomorrow night at Cruger's," he reminded her, hopping back onto the deck of his cruiser. "I'll see you at nine."

"Thanks be praised, you're back." Sister Marian thrust a fussy Amanda into Kristen's arms, then collapsed in a heap in the only chair the small room provided, a shabby green stuffed recliner on shaky legs.

"I'm sorry I took so long." Kristen kissed her daughter's cheek. She noticed Amanda's swollen eyes and runny nose. "Amanda, sweetheart, you know Mommy always comes back. There's no need to cry."

Amanda rubbed her eyes with her tiny fists, then slumped against her mother's shoulder.

"She's such a beautiful child." Sister Marian angled her head and peered at Kristen for a long minute. "You look like you're ready to collapse in a heap. You're nearly asleep on your feet. You need ten hours on your back in that bed."

"I'm fine," Kristen insisted, refusing to let her exhaustion slow her down. At the most, she had only a few days at the shelter, then she'd need to relocate. Staying in one place too long wouldn't be smart. "Did you speak to Mother Ramose about me staying another day or two?"

"You can stay as long as you like, dear. That's never been an issue." Sister Marian glanced at the clock. "I feel I need to warn you, however, about staying out this late in Algiers. The streets aren't safe after dark."

"I appreciate your concern. But if I'm going to change things for me and Amanda, I'm going to have to take a few risks." The conversation reminded Kristen that she'd made a promise to the Blu Devil to meet him tomorrow night. "I have to go out again tomorrow evening. It could get late."

Sister Marian arched one of her dark eyebrows. "Well, I've warned you. Now all I can do is pray that God has a spare angel with time on his hands to watch over you."

"He?" Kristen smiled and reached out to pat the nun's arm. "I believe I already have my angel. You've been very kind to us. I can't tell you how much I appreciate it."

Sister Marian blushed. "You, dear girl, are as beautiful as you are brave. Your mother must be very proud of you."

The comment was unexpected, but Kristen kept her focus. She had lied to Sister Marian. She'd said she was searching for her father who had abandoned her and her mother years ago. She hadn't revealed her loss of memory, or that she was on the run from Salva. She'd just needed a strong enough reason to allow her and Amanda to stay at the shelter. An abandoned family in search of the bastard father who had run out on them seemed like the perfect excuse to be asking the shelter for sanctuary. And it had worked—the shelter had welcomed them with open arms.

"So you'll stay with Amanda tomorrow night?" Kristen asked.

"Tomorrow it's my turn to lead the evening praise service. It usually lasts until eight, sometimes eight-thirty."

"I can't take Amanda with me. He can't know about—" Kristen snapped her mouth shut.

"What was that? Are you speaking about that wild Blu Devil again? Do you really think he has information about your father?"

"Yes, I do." Hating the way she had to continue to lie, Kristen changed the subject. "Were you able to get me a phone book?"

"It's on your nightstand." Sister Marian stood, then pointed to the thick directory where it sat on the tattered little table. "I'll let you rest now, and see you in the morning at breakfast. And don't worry about tomorrow night. As soon as I can, I'll be back to watch Amanda for you."

Hours after Sister Marian had left, Kristen was still up. Amanda was asleep on the narrow bed, but she was seated in the chair with the phone directory in her lap, scanning the pages in hopes that a name would spark her memory. All she needed was one name—any name—that would become a small clue as to who she was and where she belonged.

Kristen was still going through the lists of names at 4:00 a.m.

Chapter 6

Cruger's was always crowded on Friday nights, and noisy, too. But when the screen door swung open, then slammed shut, the noise settled and heads turned to watch the Blu Devil saunter through the door in his usual attire of faded jeans and a black sleeveless T-shirt. What followed was at least a dozen offers to pay for his beer and share a table—a year ago, no one would have offered him squat. Just look what a few newspaper articles could do for a man's image, Blu thought with disgust.

He declined the offers, waved a few genuine friends off with a nod, and dismissed the three women bunched together at the bar who were anxiously waiting to be asked upstairs. In truth, since he'd made the decision to work for Patch, the only sex he could round up was the kind he had to pay for. But it had been weeks since he'd used an upstairs room.

Dismissing the women, Blu limped to the far end of

the bar and hooked his backside onto a stool. Nate Cruger, the establishment's owner, stood behind the bar, both hands moving in two different directions. He'd been serving beer and gossip to his customers for over thirty years and he was the best in the business at both. With *Oui, mon ami,* and a smile quickly following, he slid a beer bottle in Blu's direction while he kept one ear on Billy-Bob LaRoux whining about his girlfriend's old man, and his free hand ringing up Spoon Thompson's tab.

When Spoon spied Blu, he stuffed the change into his pocket and came to stand beside him. "You want to find a table and talk over my offer, duFray? I've been rethinking the money end of it and—"

"And it won't be enough, Thompson. You can't afford me."

Spoon shook his head. "Now, Blu, I don't think that's true. I'm willing to—"

Blu turned his head barely an inch and evil-eyed Spoon into silence. "Go away, Thompson. We don't have anything to talk about."

When Blu released the older man from his devil's stare, he tipped up his beer bottle and took a healthy swig. He heard Spoon swear, then out of the corner of his eye, he saw him back up—right into a drunk who had staggered to the bar to pay for the pleasure of his condition. The drunk lost his balance and fell to the floor. When Blu saw who was beneath Spoon's feet, he took a second look. Perch Aldwin—drunk? That was a surprise.

He knew Perch had hit on hard times—only yesterday Spoon had said that his business had gone belly-up. But falling-down drunk didn't fit Perch Aldwin. He'd been raised on principles and the idea that hard work fixed everything. Or fast fists and no conscience, Blu thought with a sardonic grunt that was directed at himself more than anyone else.

As Perch grumbled his displeasure from his sprawled position on the floor, Spoon Thompson laughed, then gave the downed man a kick before stepping over him. Blu watched as Perch groaned, then tried to get up. On the third try, he gave up and laid there. Blu waited to see if someone was going to be a good-ol'-Joe and help him out. When no one made an effort, he slid off his bar stool and hauled the old man to his feet. Since Perch was too rubber-legged to stay vertical, he shouldered him and headed out the back door.

In the alley, Blu propped Perch against the brick wall, then backed off. When the older man finally focused on who it was who had come to his aid, he started swinging his arms. "Get away from me, you no-good evil bastard. You got no reason to come after me. Not anymore, you don't."

"I'm not hassling you, old man. I'm not in that line of work any longer. You want me to call somebody to pick you up? Curt?"

"Go to hell, you black-haired devil. Don't owe nobody nothing anymore. Ain't got nothing no more."

They were old enemies, and Blu knew that Perch would forever remember the night he had put his grandson in the hospital. He eyed the scar over the old man's graying brow, knowing every time he faced this man, he would be reminded of who he had been once upon a desperate time.

Realizing there was nothing he could say to make Perch feel better, to make himself feel better, Blu left the old man in the alley and went back inside. Seated at the bar once more, he slipped Billy-Bob LaRoux twenty bucks to drive Perch Aldwin home, then checked his watch.

It was after nine, and Blu was beginning to think Angel wasn't going to show. He would be annoyed if that was the case, but not worried. Last night he'd followed her after dropping her off at DuBay Pier, and he'd learned she was staying at the Catholic women's shelter on Carmel Avenue.

He didn't want to have to run her down, though. It was crazy, but he wanted her to come looking for him, as she'd done before. He wanted to see her step into the bar and scan the room full of faces until she found him. He wanted her to come to him a step at a time, wanted to watch it happen.

Wanted her to *trust* him.

Hell, he was wanting too much from a little *fille* he barely knew. That wasn't the Blu Devil's style—wanting what you couldn't pay for, or didn't deserve.

He glanced at the door as it opened, disappointed when he saw it wasn't her. He wished he had mentioned someplace a little less busy for them to meet. Cruger's was packed on weekends and he should have considered that. And if that wasn't bad enough, the crowd was mostly men. With what Angel had gone through in the past three years, she didn't need to be meeting him in a barroom full of rowdy, obnoxious men. Especially since the men viewed the women who frequented Cruger's in the same light as the three easy females at the other end of the bar.

When Angel finally showed up, she was forty minutes late and Blu was on his fifth beer, two over his limit—a limit he'd set for himself not because he didn't enjoy drinking, but because excess often led to reckless behavior he usually regretted later, or couldn't afford financially.

He pushed away from the bar, forgetting all about waiting for her to come to him. Relieved to see her, and at the same time annoyed as hell that she'd kept him waiting, he crossed to the door, took hold of her arm, and steered her toward an empty table at the back of the room. Without a word, he jerked the chair out and put her on it. Then he reached for a chair close by and straddled it, wedging her into the corner, forgetting about her fear of big men and being manhandled.

"You're late," he snapped. "Where the hell have you been? I said nine o'clock."

"Nine didn't work."

Blu eyed her hair, suddenly realizing that half the length was gone. "Where is it?"

"Where's what?"

"Your hair, dammit."

"I feel better if I keep changing my looks in case Salva—" She stopped herself. "It's a wig."

Blu eyed the wig. "So you think Maland's out looking for you."

"I don't think. I know he's looking for me." She laid her small bag on the table, opened it and pulled out the photos. Handing them to him, she said, "The first four are me, the other two are you. The ones of me aren't recent." She leaned toward him and Blu caught a whiff of lemon. "See, my hair is short in that one. These were taken before I met Salva because I've worn my hair to my waist for two years. Salva insists."

Her last comment made Blu take his eyes from the picture to stare at her. "What do you mean, he insists?"

"Like he insists all the men working for him wear

his tattoo, the women wear their hair long and straight.''

A control freak, Blu decided. A twisted crazy who likes to play power games. He kept his thoughts to himself and shuffled to the next picture.

''See, my hair's the same in that one. That's a Sandpiper there, and I'm standing near—''

''Hold it.'' Blu jerked his head up again. ''A Sandpiper? You know what kind of boat this is?''

''Yes. But I don't know why I know that.''

Blu rubbed his jaw, then handed her the next picture. ''And what do you see in this picture?''

She studied the snapshot. ''The background is blurred, but behind the dock I'm standing on I think that's an old pilothouse. It looks like it's from the seventies. They were broad like that, and top-heavy.'' She looked up. ''Is that what you wanted me to tell you?''

Blu didn't know what he'd wanted her to tell him, but suddenly his curiosity doubled.

''Blu?''

It was the first time she had left *devil* off his name. ''Yeah?''

''What do you think it means, these things I know?''

''It means you haven't forgotten everything about your past. You must have spent time around a marina. Yesterday, on the Gulf, you were as seaworthy and comfortable as I was on the *Nightwing*. You know boats and you've been on water a lot.''

She was smiling now—sure they'd just discovered a piece of the puzzle. Her smile was so damn sweet that Blu felt his inside turn to mush. Never having felt anything like it, he quickly went back to examining the pictures, examining a younger version of the woman who sat beside him. She had the same innocent eyes, the same sun-bleached hair, only short enough that her ears and slender neck were exposed. She looked maybe fifteen—her tank top revealed a slight swell to her teenage breasts, and her short cutoffs accenting a hint of curve to her maturing hips.

Blu set down the pictures. "You said you're twenty-four?"

"And you said it's a lie."

He examined her delicate features, her smooth flawless skin. "I think you think it's a lie, too."

She broke eye contact, stared at the scarred table surface. "Salva's older," she confessed. "He celebrated his thirty-ninth birthday a month ago. Why would an older man be attracted to someone so much younger?"

Blu stiffened. Why indeed.

"If we met three years ago and I'm not twenty, then—"

"Then he's got a lot of explaining to do." Blu's tone was full of disgust.

Her head shot up. "No! I don't want to see him again. Not ever." Suddenly she was gripping Blu's arm in the same frantic manner she had yesterday when she'd thought he was going to turn her over to Jackson at the apartment building. "Promise me I won't ever have to face him. I don't ever want him touching me again, Blu. Oh, God, please. Please, Blu, if he finds me, he'll—"

"Take it easy." Blu covered her hand with his. "If he shows up—"

She pulled her hand away from his. "If he shows up, I'm dead. Do you get that? Dead. Or may as well be."

Her fear was real and it bothered him. Oh, hell, there

it was—the Crescent City Devil had started to grow a conscience. Blu picked up the pictures and quickly flipped through them to single out the one of Angel he liked the best—the one where her eyes were as bright as her smile—then handed the others back. "I'll keep this one."

"Why?"

"There's a chance I might be able to locate the pier, or the boat. I'll check it out."

The reason for pocketing the picture was lame, but it was the best he could do short of telling her the truth. And right now Blu wasn't too happy with the truth. He didn't need a conscience messing with his thinking and muddying up the water.

"Then taking the photos was a good idea. It could be a clue. We might be able to find that pilothouse and then—"

"Whoa!" Blu stuck the picture in the pocket of his black T-shirt. "Don't get your heart set on a miracle happening. This is a long shot at best."

The comment, as well as his chiding tone, was like dousing her with ice water. Suddenly she was no longer smiling. "Long shots are better than nothing. Now, if you'll excuse me, I'd like to use the rest room. Where is it?"

"Down the hall, left of the bar." Blu had to physically stand and move his chair to let her out of the corner. When she headed in the direction he'd pointed, he spun the chair around and sat. As she sauntered away from him in her trim jeans and blouse, he studied her, deciding if she was going to change her looks, she'd need to do more than simply buy a wig a shade darker than her original hair color and shorten it by a foot.

After she'd disappeared, Blu found himself tapping his fingers on the table, already anxious for her to come back to him. He scanned the bar crowd. Cruger's was a small joint, easy to see everyone in the place at a quick glance, and he knew them all. The bar itself consisted of plain wood tables and mismatched chairs. There was no decor to speak of—men didn't appreciate that sort of thing, anyway, and knowing that, Nate Cruger had been smart enough to put his money into the one thing customers did care about, good beer.

A long five minutes lapsed. When Angel didn't return, Blu checked his watch. Wondering if she was sick, or if she'd simply taken off, he got up and headed down the hall that led to the unisex rest room.

Seeing the door was closed, he was just about to knock when he heard a scuffle followed by a faint cry. A split second later one solid kick sent the door flying inward. Two seconds later Blu was inside reaching for Sam Miller—a welder he recognized from the docks—who had Angel pinned against the sink, groping her with greedy fingers. He didn't say a word as he threw the inebriated man face-first into the wall. Blood ran from the man's nose, but Blu ignored it as he drove his fist into his stomach, then into his jaw. The sound of bones breaking was sickening, and the doomed man dropped to his knees.

Still enraged, Blu grabbed Sam by the shirt and lifted him back to his rubbery legs. His fist was poised and nearly on its way to break another bone when Angel cried out for him to stop. He spun around to find her clinging to the far wall, her eyes wide with fear, her face ghostly pale. A second later she was bolting for the door, scrambling through the curious crowd that had jam-packed the hall.

"Angel!" Blu let the near-unconscious man slump to the floor and raced after her. By the time he elbowed his way out of Cruger's, she had more than a block headstart on him.

The buttons had been torn from her blouse. Kristen tugged the edges together to cover her white bra, and sprinted down the alley. She turned the block before the women's shelter and ducked into yet another dark alley to catch her breath.

She desperately wanted to go back to the shelter, but not with her clothes torn and her body shaking with fear. She didn't want her daughter to see her this way, and not Sister Marian, either.

Kristen still didn't know how she could have entered the bathroom without seeing that creep lurking in the corner. It wasn't until she'd locked herself in that she'd spied him grinning at her. She released a shudder, recalling the moment he attacked her. She had tried to fight him off, had prayed for someone to come to her rescue. And then Blu had appeared with his fists clenched and his anger raging and…suddenly she'd been transported back to the island where—more than once—she'd been forced to watch Salva beat the life out of a guard or brutalize some poor gardener.

Yes, in that moment Blu had become Salva, and in those terrifying seconds she'd panicked.

Kristen knew the situation was completely different. Blu was there to help her, not hurt her. But the moment had twisted on her and it had snapped her back to the island in the blink of an eye. Embarrassed now that she had run, she stepped out of the alley. She had to find a change of clothes, and then she had to get back to the shelter before something else crazy happened.

A small shop at the end of the street still had its lights on. The name over the door read Spirit World. Kristen hurried to the door and stepped inside the cluttered little shop in hopes of finding a replacement for her ruined blouse.

As she scanned her surroundings, she saw an array of voodoo dolls, incense, candles, and various effigies. Optimistic that she would find something in the line of clothing, she headed down a narrow aisle. Overhead, and along the outer walls, hundreds of wooden masks stared at her. The masks were crudely made, some depicting animals, others, human. Then there were creative combinations of both. Strangely enough, the masks didn't intimidate her. She knew that the house-blessing masks were as commonplace in New Orleans as seafood gumbo.

They were?

Again Kristen was aware that she'd remembered something she apparently knew as fact, but not how or why. She glanced around, studying the masks. It was strange, but she felt almost at home with these masks. A strange kind of kinship.

The sweet scent of opium incense clung in the air. And the scent seemed as familiar to Kristen as the house-blessing masks. Her own favorite scent, lemon verbena, could be found in shops such as this.

She continued to move through the aisles until she came to a gauze-draped doorway in the back. There were voices coming from behind the curtain, a strong female voice and a deep baritone. Kristen crept closer, peeked along the open side of the curtain. A woman sat at a small round table, her face young and beautiful, her dark intelligent eyes outlined with colorful glitter. Her lips were a ripe red. As she moved her dark curly head and began to chant, the large gold hoops at her ears glistened in the lamplight.

Kristen feigned interest in one of the masks next to the door so she could linger without suspicion. Eavesdropping was something she'd gotten good at while living with Salva. She had always felt like a houseguest in what was suppose to be her own home, and the only way she'd learned anything had been by listening in on conversations.

That's how she'd discovered that her mother-in-law hated her. It was also how she'd found out that Salva had a brother he spoke to once a week on the phone. It's how she'd learned that every guard, maid and nanny who worked for her husband did so out of fear, not loyalty. It's also how she'd come to realize that "the business" her husband operated was of an illegal nature. No wonder he hadn't cared if she was a fugitive—her husband was one himself.

The chanting stopped and the woman began to use tarot cards to tell the man's future. Absorbed in the woman's hands as she turned over the cards one by one, Kristen didn't hear the outside door open, or see the man who slipped inside. And it was only after she sensed someone behind her that the hair on the back of her neck stood out.

With her heart climbing her throat, she slowly turned to find the Blu Devil less than a foot away. On instinct, she clutched her torn blouse to her breasts and took a step back.

He said, "We don't have time for you to act up, so don't. You're being tailed, and we can expect the guy in the next minute or two."

"Guy?"

"That's what I said. He's a *hulk* wearing leather. Sound familiar?"

"No."

"Come on. We need to get out of here."

Kristen spun around, looking for a way to escape the little shop. There appeared to be no way out, not unless there was a back entrance beyond the curtain.

The front door opened and in walked the Hulk. "Oh, God." Kristen slumped against Blu and immediately started to shake. The man was very large. But that wasn't the worst of it—the Hulk had a bald head.

Salva's shaved head hadn't been all that odd. Even though he could grow plenty of thick, dark hair, his choice to shave his shiny pate daily had never prompted Kristen to ask why. But what she had always thought was odd was her husband's insistence that all the men who worked for him shave their heads, too, as well as wear the dagger tattoo in their palm. The only people on the Maland estate who were allowed to keep their hair were the women. And as she'd already told Blu, they couldn't cut an inch off without Salva's approval.

"Do you recognize him?"

Kristen focused on the man's face. "No, I don't know him," she whispered, her voice full of fear. "But he works for Salva."

"How do you know that?"

"He has a bald head." Kristen's voice broke. "They all have bald heads."

She had stepped closer to Blu—almost huddling against him—and now as she gazed up at him, she found him looking at her strangely. She knew it was a crazy thing to say, but unless you'd been on the island to see how many bald-headed men worked for her husband it was impossible to understand the magnitude of her statement.

"Come on." Blu parted the curtain and forced Kristen ahead of him into the back room. The psychic looked up, alarmed at first, but when her gaze traveled past Kristen, a smile parted her bloodred lips. "*Bonjour,* my sweet devil."

Blu nodded, then spoke to the woman in rapid French. Suddenly she wasn't smiling anymore, but standing quickly and ushering the man who had been seated at her table out of the room, telling him she would be back with him momentarily.

Returning, she pulled on the side of a bookcase. "Inside, quickly."

Kristen peered into the darkness, afraid to move. She heard Blu say, *"Merci, Lema,"* before he shoved her into the small space and followed. In an instant they were sandwiched together behind the bookcase in the darkness.

Kristen reached out and felt the walls on all three sides. She turned, bumped into Blu's hard chest. "This is nothing more than a closet," she snapped. "We're trapped."

"Shh! Quiet."

He shifted and suddenly his entire length was pressed tightly to Kristen. She tried to step back, but there was no room to spare. She was about to insist that he get them out of there when she heard a man call out to Lema.

"*Mais,* yeah, *m'sieu.* I'll be right there."

If one of Salva's men had found her this quickly, that meant her husband had connections everywhere. Was it true, then? Could Salva snatch her back to the island in a blink of an eye? Was she forever *his* as he'd told her every day for the past three years? Would she never know who she really was, where she belonged?

Kristen started to shake. She didn't want to confront the Hulk, but she didn't want to remain in this black box, either—especially since the closet wasn't big enough for one broom—a skinny broom, at that. She'd never been claustrophobic before, but this was suddenly reminding her of a recurring nightmare she'd been having since leaving the island—the one where she found herself drowning in blackness. So much blackness.

For three days she'd gone without sleep afraid to close her eyes.

"Easy, Angel." His lips touched her ear at the same time his hands slid over her shoulders and squeezed gently. "I can feel you shaking. Don't fall apart on me."

She could feel his stone-hard thighs pressed against her hips, feel his chest moving with each breath he took, feel his body heat growing, spreading. Consuming hers. "I'm afraid," she admitted.

"Of being in here with me, or the guy outside?"

It was a fair question. Kristen wanted to say both, but the truth was, as nervous as she was about being in this tight spot with Blu, it didn't compare to the fear of being captured and taken back to Salva. "I can't go back," she whispered, desperation in her voice.

"We can trust Lema. She won't give us up."

"She might not have to. That man looks capable of tearing this place apart a board at a time if he thinks I'm here." As she said the words, dread filled Kristen and she knew what the Hulk's presence meant—Salva had locked in on her location. He was coming for her. Coming for Amanda.

Amanda... Oh, God. Did Salva know where she was?

"Do you think this man knows where I've been staying?" she whispered.

"No, or he wouldn't be so persistent now. He'd just sit back and wait for you to go back to the women's shelter."

"The shelter? You know where I've been staying?"

"I followed you last night."

Kristen felt her world tilt. The room suddenly turned hot and her heart began to pound. She felt her head start to spin and she let go of her torn blouse and clasped Blu's arms in a white-knuckled grip. "I can't breathe."

"Easy."

Blu's body was pressed so tight to her, Kristen could feel the strength in his treelike stature. She leaned back, bracing her head against the wall, trying to gain some distance. The sound of voices on the other side caused a whimper to escape her lips and she gripped Blu's solid arms tighter.

"Concentrate on something else," he drawled.

Eyes squeezed shut, Kristen tried to chase away her growing panic. "I can't, it's not working. Nothing's working."

"Give Lema a few minutes to get rid of him."

"If he saw me come in here he won't leave without me." Kristen was working herself into a full-fledged panic.

"Easy."

"Stop saying that."

"Shh, *fille.* Let's do something to take your mind off what's going on out there."

"And what could we possibly do? This closet isn't big enough to turn around in, much less—"

Kristen felt him shift his body, felt him press against her. Suddenly his breath brushed her cheek. She smelled a hint of beer, not sickening mint. His mouth moved closer and then he was brushing his lips over hers, taking her mind and body somewhere else.

The kiss started out whisper-soft, but in an instant the butterfly caress exploded into something reckless and wonderful. He brushed his hot lips over hers once more, then began making love to her mouth as though a firestorm had suddenly erupted inside him.

It was beyond anything Kristen had ever experienced, this poignant rush of heat, this soul-wrenching need. Fleetingly, she chastised herself for succumbing so easily to this wild, untamed kiss. Then she was sliding her hands up Blu's arms and opening her mouth wider to allow his hard, hot tongue inside.

The firestorm spread.

Engulfed by it, sexually awakened for the first time in her life, Kristen's stomach knotted. Flipped. Then flipped again. Suddenly her nipples ached and she felt an urgent need growing between her thighs. Desire was something foreign to her—at least, it had been dead for three years—and she rubbed against Blu in answer to this unexpected hunger.

The world tilted, then it didn't exist anymore as Blu pulled her away from the wall and his big hands cupped her backside and curled her more firmly against his lower body.

The black box that had become their safe haven grew smaller. Hotter. But even then, even when the Blu Devil's roused passion lay stiff and pulsing against her belly, Kristen couldn't stop her own desire, or the longing this man's heat ignited.

It was the first, she mused. The first time she had ever lost herself in a man's kiss, to his hot touch. At least, that she remembered.

Chapter 7

He wasn't going to mention the kiss. And since *she* had refused to even look at him since they'd left Lema's, Blu figured it was safe to say the entire episode was going to die a slow death—a very slow death because he was still smoldering from the waist down.

The kiss had been a way to keep her quiet. He'd acted before he'd thought. No, that wasn't true. He'd been dying to kiss her. Only he'd never expected her to give back the way she had. He'd never expected her to feed the fire that had sent him so quickly out of control.

"You're sure he didn't follow us?"

She sounded a little breathless, tired of the pace he'd set. Blu didn't break his stride as he ushered her onto DuBay Pier where the *Nightwing* rode the gentle tide. "I can't guarantee that. But we're not going to stick around and find out."

She stopped. ''Meaning?''

Blu spun around. ''Meaning, we don't have time for this right now. We're shipping out.'' He started walking again, hoping she would follow. He'd give her fifteen seconds and then she'd be over his shoulder whether she liked it or not. He heard her start after him. She was smart, he'd give her that. Hell, he'd give her more than that; that little mouth of hers could be the CIA's best secret weapon if they ever found out about it. He'd never experienced so much localized heat storming his groin all at once in his entire life.

His body hadn't wanted to stop, and even the night air wasn't doing much to settle him down. The sight of Angel dressed in one of Lema's sarongs wasn't helping, either. In the moonlight, even in the wig, she looked like some erotic sea witch he'd pulled from the ocean. But it was over now, and to remind himself of that fact, he noticed she had grown as skittish as a cornered spider crab. With good reason, he admitted. Things had gone too far in that closet, he'd touched her in places he shouldn't have. Hell, fully clothed, he'd damn near made love to her in a two-by-two closet.

When they reached the cruiser, he hurried aboard, then turned to help her over the side. Only there was no need, she leaped onto the cruiser's deck with seasoned agility, again reminding him that she was no novice where boats were concerned. Not even the red-and-purple, ankle-length sarong affected her deft coordination.

It made him question himself another time. Did he know her? Was he supposed to? If she had lived in the area three years ago when would he have met her? Where? He studied the sarong and how it outlined her curves. Three years ago she would have been fifteen or sixteen. Seventeen at the oldest.

While she had changed into the sarong, he'd glimpsed more bruises on her body. He'd agreed to step out of the curtained room, but as she'd turned her back to shed her ruined blouse, he had watched her through the open edge of the curtain. He'd seen dark marks along her fragile rib cage and the length of her spine.

"Is that you, Blu?"

The call came from below deck. Blu answered, "It's me. Get on up here, *mon ami.*"

"Who's that?"

For the first time since they'd left Lema's, Angel was looking him straight in the eye. "That's Mort," he told her. "He works for me, and sleeps on the cruiser sometimes."

Mort scaled the stairs two at a time. The teenager was sixteen, as thin as Angel and no more than two inches taller. But the experience that showed brightly in his clear blue eyes made him look much older, and years wiser. "What's up?" he asked.

"I want you to bunk in with Brodie for a few days." Blu glanced toward the waterfront. There was still no one in sight, but he wasn't willing to take any chances.

Mort cocked his head and eyed Angel. "Who's she?"

"Never mind." Blu's voice bit hard as his gaze locked on Mort once more. "Just round up your stuff and take off."

Mort grinned. ''Not a problem. I'll be out of your hair in five minutes.'' Good at his word, in record time the teenager was back on deck with a small duffel bag slung over his shoulder.

''Tell Brodie, until he hears from me, he's in charge of the fleet.''

Mort leaped to the dock, then spun around. ''Why?''

''Never mind why. Tell him I might be out as long as a week.''

''A week!'' Mort glanced at Angel once more, then back to Blu again. ''You've never taken any days off since...since we met.''

''Well, I'm taking some days now.''

It was true his routine for the past eight years had been well established, but Blu didn't question his decision, and he didn't like Mort questioning him, either. ''Hightail it so I can shove off.''

Once Mort was gone, Blu turned and found Angel glaring at him. ''What?''

''You were rude to him.''

''We need to get moving.'' Blu untied the boat from its moorings.

''Do you always boss people around?''

''I've never given it much thought.'' Blu headed for the helm.

''Well, maybe you should.''

''This is my boat.'' He turned over the engine. ''I'm the boss.''

''You're not the boss of me,'' she snapped.

Blu turned to look at her. ''At the moment, I'll have to disagree.''

''Because you're bigger and stronger?''

Blu backed the cruiser away from the pier. "Can we talk about this later? Right now we need to get out of here." With that, he left the pier behind with a burst of speed. "We won't go far," he called over his shoulder, "there's a place at River Bay. It's about a mile from here."

Ten minutes later, Blu nosed the *Nightwing* into a congested marina overrun with boats in all shapes and sizes—from sailboats to houseboats to luxury yachts. "There's only a handful of people who would look for me here," he told her, mooring the boat to the dock. "But no one you need to worry about."

She was at the railing, searching the quiet maze of boats docked around them. "Do you think Salva's man contacted him?" She faced him. "Do you think they're searching for me right now?"

The growing fear in her eyes was hard to watch. "We can't be sure that guy got a good look at you. But there's no sense taking chances. You'll need to stay out of sight for a while. And this is a good place. Finding someone here is next to impossible, that is unless you know what you're looking for. And they don't." Blu double checked the ropes that secured them to the dock. When he turned back, he caught Angel scanning the waterfront with more interest than he thought she should. "Don't be stupid," he warned. "This is a perfect hiding place for you."

"Is it, really?"

"Yes."

She was suddenly looking at him with accusing eyes. "What? Why *that* look?" he asked.

"That man in the bathroom tonight. It was almost

as if… It looked like… Hitting him seemed to come easy. Was it?"

He hadn't expected her to bring that up. "It felt right," Blu hedged. "I hit Sam because he was all over you and he deserved to pay for it."

She looked as if she wanted to believe him, but then a half hour ago he had been all over her, too. The irony almost choked him.

"You knew him?"

"He's one of the welders down on the docks." Blu rubbed at his jaw, studied her some more. "You weren't exactly enjoying his attentions, as I recall."

"No. No, I wasn't."

"Then I don't see why we're discussing this."

"You didn't enjoy it, then? Hurting him, I mean?"

Of course he enjoyed sinking his fist into that bastard's face and sending him to his knees. But that's not what she wanted to hear, and the way she was looking at him…

Oh, hell, his conscience was growing. "No, Angel. I didn't enjoy it. I just wanted him off you." Hoping that would suffice, he said, "It's late. Past midnight. You need to get some sleep."

"Sleep? No, I really—"

"You look tired."

"I haven't been sleeping well. I've been having nightmares."

Blu strolled across the deck, opened the door that led below, then gestured to the stairs. "I've got two beds. You can have your own room. I'll bet once you stretch out you'll fall right to sleep."

The *Nightwing* was called "The Charmer" by the local fishermen. She was forty-five feet of sleek design and unchallenged speed. In a class by herself, the *Nightwing,* however, didn't stop with surface beauty and speed. Below deck, the well-crafted cruiser had a roomy U-shaped galley and generous living space, and was equipped with two private sleeping quarters, each with their own head.

In comparison to the Dump, the cruiser was a floating mansion, well-cared for and cleaner than anyone would expect.

"This is a surprise," she said as she came to stand in the teakwood galley.

Blu glanced around. "She was custom-made for a guy over on Lake Borgne. When he died, his wife put her up for sale. She's a one-of-a-kind."

"And yours?"

"*Oui,* she's mine."

Blu watched Angel as she considered the space with an experienced eye of someone who knew what she was looking at. "I know it's weird, but I feel comfortable here. Like maybe I used to live on a boat or something." She ran her hand along the teakwood cabinets. Suddenly she closed her eyes as if she were trying to remember. For several minutes she just stood there.

Blu came up behind her, but made a point to not touch her. "Do you remember something?"

She blinked open her eyes, turned to face him. "I wish I did, but no. There's nothing." As if the ordeal of trying to remember had stripped her of her last ounce of energy, she stepped around him and sank onto the sofa bench that hugged the table on three sides.

Blu retrieved a glass from the cupboard and ran water into it at the sink. "Here. You hungry?"

"No."

He slid the glass onto the table and she stared at it for a long time before reaching for it. He said, "You trying to decide whether it's clean or not?"

"No. But now that you mention it, this place is quite a change from your apartment building."

"It's going to take more than a little bit of cash to fix up the Dump and turn it into a house. Like I told Jackson, I'll get to it eventually. But there's more important things sucking my back pockets dry at the moment."

"Like your fishing boats?"

"The duFray Devils are more than just boats. They're a legend. To retire the fleet or sell them out would be a crime. More than thirty men and their families depend on that fleet. That's not to mention my mother's fish market, and a dozen others like it."

She took a sip of water. "So the Blu Devil isn't as tough and heartless as his name implies."

Blu scowled at her. "What's that supposed to mean?"

"Only that your concern is puzzling. You care about your crew and your mother. But Sister Marian warned me that—"

"Listen to her. I'm no saint."

"I won't argue with that, and I'm sure that man in the bathroom tonight won't either." She set the glass aside, yawned, then crossed her arms on the table and laid her head on top of them. "I'm going to rest here for just a bit," she mumbled.

Blu ambled down the hall to the spare bedroom to see what shape Mort had left it in. Disappointed, he decided to give Angel his room for the night.

"You ready to turn in?" He had come back into the kitchen and was standing a foot away from where she sat resting her head on folded arms. Her eyes were closed, but he hadn't been gone five minutes. She couldn't be asleep. Not that quick. Could she?

"Angel?" When she didn't answer, Blu hunkered down to study her face. She was sleeping, all right—her breathing was slow and even.

He reached up and pulled the wig off her head and watched as her long blond hair tumbled over her bare shoulders and into her lap. Groaning, he drawled, "*Bon Dieu!* But you're beautiful, *fille.*"

He stood slowly, his groin pulsing with the sweet memory of how good she'd felt against him while they had been in Lema's closet. Frustrated, Blu returned to his bedroom and threw back the sheet, turned the light on that hung on the wall above the bed, then back-tracked to the galley. Careful to not wake her, he lifted her into his arms and moved down the hall as light-footed as he could. In his bedroom, he gently laid her on the wide, built-in teakwood bed, then removed her shoes one at a time.

She had slender legs, delicate ankles and feet with narrow arches. Her toenails, Blu discovered, were painted a soft pink.

He set her deck shoes on the floor and as he turned back, she was stretching in her sleep. A moment later she was lifting one small arm high above her head, revealing the bruises above her elbow.

Reminded once more of what she'd been through, Blu wondered if there were more bruises elsewhere. His curiosity piqued, he reached down and parted the colorful sarong to expose her legs.

Though he enjoyed feasting his eyes on her beautiful legs, the best part was not finding anymore bruises. Relieved, he inched the sarong higher and uncovered a pair of nude-colored lace panties that showed off her flat belly and sexy little navel. The narrow V where her legs came together caught his attention. She was so damn petite and tiny that the idea of what kind of patience and restraint it would take to make love to her made him wince.

She shifted, bent a sexy knee. It caused her legs to part slightly, exposing aging black bruises high on the inside of her legs. Blu frowned, then leaned over to examine the discoloration, as well as the size and position of the marks. A connoisseur of bruises, he knew exactly what he was looking at—someone had forced her legs apart, gripping and pinching at the same time. The angle of the hands and the separate finger definitions put *that someone* over top of her. Blu estimated that it had happened no more than four or five days ago.

Rage flared inside him, and in that same moment his past and the present collided head-on. He gulped air, tried to shake off the irony of it all. His own greed had put him in the business of brutalizing people to fix his own mistake. He'd felt justified because he'd made the excuse that he was saving the duFray Devils. But he was no better than Salvador Maland—hurting someone to get what he wanted, to keep what he wanted.

Blu swore silently. If he was a superstitious sort, he would say someone was toying with his mind to get even for his past transgressions. And there was sure something to that. Lema would remind him that in the spirit world all things were possible. She would remind him of the time he had come to her and she had called upon Agwe, the voodoo sea god, to watch over his aging fleet. A request that had not been ignored—how else could he explain his ships returning to port safely day after day, their hulls full of shrimp, his crew healthy? His repairs minor?

A sour taste in his mouth, Blu covered Angel with the sheet and left the room feeling a jumble of emotions: rage, revulsion for the man he'd become, disgust for lusting after an innocent. He'd been all over her like…like he wanted to climb inside her, as if he had the right to taste perfection. A man like him. *Bon Dieu!*

Feeling like a hypocrite, Blu stood topside and watched as a band of dark thunderheads swallowed up the sky. The wind had picked up, and the high-masted sailboats on either side of him swayed and groaned with each sudden gust. But tucked safely within the sheltered berth of the larger boats, the *Nightwing* rode safe as a newborn babe in a cradle.

He smelled the rain before he felt it, but it didn't chase him below deck—he had too much thinking to do, too much guilt to swallow.

A half hour later, soaked clean through, Blu turned away from the railing, his decision made. Patch Pollaro knew people in low places and if anyone could find out the skinny on a scumbag named Salvador Maland, it was another scumbag. It was the right thing to do, he decided—to pay a visit to his old boss. Then why did he feel as though his life had just taken a giant step backward?

The old nightmare had a new twist. Kristen was drowning. But she wasn't drowning alone, someone else was there with her. Someone who wasn't going to make it back to the boat.

The fear in those green eyes, the terror....

Kristen cried out, tried to go back and help. The water was so cold and the waves so angry and unforgiving.

No, *he* wasn't going to make it, and she couldn't reach him.

"Ben! No! Ben, noooo—"

"Angel?"

"No, Ben. Ben, please!"

"Angel, wake up."

Kristen snapped her eyes open and found herself staring into the scowling face of the Blu Devil. The next thing that registered was that he was all wet, a green towel curled around his neck. No, he wasn't just wet, he was soaked.

"What's happening? What's wrong?" She scrambled up into a sitting position.

"You tell me. Who's Ben?"

"Ben?" Kristen shook her head. "I don't know. Why are you all wet?"

"We've got a storm kicking up."

"It's raining?"

He nodded. "I was topside for a while. You were calling for Ben. Another nightmare?"

"Yes." Kristen shoved the sheet aside and hugged her knees. The white sheets were surprisingly clean, the built-in bungalow was cozy and it smelled like… "Is this room yours?"

"Yeah."

"I thought you said there were two rooms."

"Mort's stuff is all over the spare. He must have thought we were going to— I already planned on taking the other room, but if you prefer to stay there, I'll—"

"No. This is fine."

He turned away, tossed the towel on the floor, then stripped off his wet T-shirt. "Tell me about this nightmare."

"I was drowning in the Gulf." His muscular torso caught Kristen's eye. Not wanting to stare, she began to study the room. She heard a noise, and she turned to see Blu rummaging in one of his drawers. Her gaze traveled the length of his broad back, then lower to where his wet jeans hugged his butt and long legs. She had been going to say something, now she couldn't remember what it was.

She should look away. She should snap out of this foolish fog she'd drifted into and concentrate on the nightmare. But all she could think about was how alive she had felt when the Blu Devil wrapped her in his arms and kissed her.

In his bed, seeing him half naked, she should be clutching the sheet and reliving the déjâ vu fear that had been her life for three years. Yet as big and powerful as Blu duFray was, she wasn't afraid of him any longer. It was crazy, and she didn't completely understand why, but fear was no longer an issue.

She knew very little about kissing, but Blu duFray certainly must. The mind-numbing heat he'd offered her with his mouth had been all about giving instead of taking. And what he'd given her was still churning low and warm in her belly.

He turned and caught her staring. "Sorry. I should have... I'm just used to—"

"This is your room. It's only natural to do...uh, to do whatever it is you do in here." She'd gotten tongue-tied and it was all because she couldn't look at him without remembering the amount of heat and emotion he could fan to life by just breathing on her.

"The nightmare... We were talking about the nightmare."

"Yes." Glad he'd brought her down to earth, Kristen curled her legs beneath her in the middle of his bed, ready to tell him anything he wanted to know. Well, almost anything. She still wasn't ready to expose Amanda to anyone. "I've had trouble sleeping in the past. Dr. Eden gave me a prescription to help me relax."

"Sleeping pills?"

"Yes. He called it a mild sedative."

"Do you have them on you?"

"No. I stopped taking them the night I left the house."

"And you've had trouble sleeping since?"

"Yes."

"You called out to Ben. Got any idea who he is?"

He hung one hand on his hip, the other held a pair of jeans he'd retrieved from his drawer. He looked tough and dangerous, and Kristen wasn't the slightest bit afraid. "I don't have a face to put with the name, but he has green eyes. Don't you think that's strange, that I would know what color his eyes are and nothing else?" His wet jeans were making a puddle on the floor. "Maybe you should change." She motioned to the water on the floor.

He glanced down, saw the puddle. "Yeah, I suppose I should. I'll be right back."

He disappeared inside the head, limping slightly as he went. Again, Kristen found herself wondering what kind of injury had been responsible for the limp. But she didn't have long to wonder. Minutes later he was back wearing a pair of dry jeans that hugged his thighs and hard, flat belly. They were well-worn, and the contrast between the light-colored denim and his coppery chest was startling. Wonderful.

He must have been aware of her roving eyes, and to her surprise, he pulled a gray underwear tank from a drawer and slipped it on. Sitting on the edge of the bed, he asked, "Do you think you're having trouble sleeping because you don't have the sedatives with you?"

The question brought a frown to Kristen's face. She'd never given any thought to whether she'd *needed* the pills to sleep. She'd just been blaming that dreadful nightmare on the lack of them. Yes, she'd gotten used to taking the pills, mostly because they had helped her to deal with the anxiety of having to endure Salva's attention, but she'd never thought— "Oh, God! Is that why I can't sleep? Do you think I'm addicted?" When he didn't answer, Kristen stiffened. "You do, don't you? You think I'm some kind of prescription junkie!"

"Hold on," he growled. "I never said that. Don't go putting words in my mouth." He ran his hands through his wet hair, then looked at her as if he was trying to decide something.

"What? Why are you looking at me like that?"

"I was just wondering if it was intentional. If the pills were a way to control you."

She didn't dare to comment, but she knew it was true—the pills had helped her, but they had also aided Salva's sick obsession with her. The more repressed she was, the easier she had been to handle. And though he liked seeing her fear grow and her body tense with the knowledge of what would come next, there were times when she…

Kristen squeezed her eyes shut, not wanting to remember.

"What's wrong?"

"Nothing."

She felt a strong hand on her arm, and she blinked open her eyes to see that even though he'd sat as far away from her as he could get, he'd still been able to reach out and touch her. "I can't go back there," she whispered. "Please, don't ever let him touch me again. Please…"

"I promise."

He was watching her closely, knew she was feeling emotional, but instead of offering comfort, he withdrew his hand and stood. "Do you feel up to talking more about the nightmare?"

Embarrassed, Kristen pulled herself together. ''If you think it's important.''

''You said Salva's boat had the accident in the Gulf.''

''Yes.''

''In the nightmare, is everyone in the water?''

''No. Just me and Ben.''

''And the two of you are drowning?''

''Yes.''

''Why isn't Salva?''

''I don't know.''

''Try to think. What's he doing on the boat?''

Kristen did as he asked and closed her eyes, tried to think. The vision of a body floating by flashed in front of her eyes and she jerked them open and scrambled off the bed. ''He's dead. Ben's dead.'' She started to shake, then cry. She blinked back the tears but they wouldn't stop. Angry and frightened that she could cry for someone she couldn't even remember, she pounded her forehead with her small fist. ''Why can't I remember him? I know his name and that he has green eyes, so why—''

''Shh. It's okay.'' Blu tugged her into his arms and rubbed her back. ''I shouldn't have pushed. If you're supposed to remember, you will. Let's forget it for tonight.''

He let go suddenly, as if he hadn't meant to touch her in the first place. But earlier he had wanted to touch her, to hold her. Kiss her. Why was he so aloof all of a sudden? Kristen wondered.

''I've got clean T-shirts in the bottom drawer if you'd rather sleep in something else.''

"Haven't you been listening? I have nightmares when I close my eyes. I'm not sleeping anymore tonight."

"I'll bring you some warm milk." He went to the drawer, grabbed a light blue T-shirt and tossed it at her.

Angry that he was being so cold, Kristen let the T-shirt sail past her and land on the bed. "I hate warm milk."

He arched a black brow, then strolled past her, retrieved three magazines from the built-in nightstand and laid them next to the T-shirt. "Maybe if you read, you'll fall asleep. Me, I'm turning in next door."

She stared at the magazines. The top two were commercial fishing periodicals, the other… Kristen shoved the fishing mags aside and uncovered a *Playboy*. Struck speechless, she stared at the brunette with glossy red lips and monster breasts that strained to fit on the cover.

From behind her, she heard Blu swear. Then his long arm was reaching past her to snag the *Playboy*. Moments later, he was out the door, leaving her with the two fishing periodicals.

Chapter 8

Someone was singing—not singing exactly, it was more like humming. Kristen blinked awake and shoved herself up from the bed. She saw that the bedroom door was open, and wondered about that—last night Blu had closed it after he'd made his quick exit out of the room.

She flung the sheet aside and swung her legs to the floor. Wearing Blu's large T-shirt and her underwear, Kristen crept to the door and peeked out, gazing in the direction of the galley.

An older woman stood at the counter, humming while she sliced fruit. She had gray hair pulled back in a neat bun at the nape of her neck, wore flat black shoes, and a brown skirt and white blouse.

Kristen watched for a moment, keeping herself hidden, or so she thought.

"I'm Rose, Blu's mama," the woman called, not turning around.

Kristen squeezed her eyes shut for a moment, then

finally she stepped out of the bedroom and came forward. "I'm Kristen," she said. "Ah, where's Blu?"

Rose set down the knife and turned. "I was going to ask you the same thing."

Blu's mother was at least smiling. Kristen tried to relax. "I'm not sure. He never woke me, so..." She didn't finish what she was saying. It sounded as though...

"I checked DuBay Pier first thing this morning. When I didn't see the boat, I decided I might find him here. He uses the old family slip here at River Bay sometimes when there's a storm brewing. Last night we had a corker. Relax, child. I normally don't waltz in like this unannounced. I had some news for my son, and when he didn't hear me call down, I thought he might be sick or something."

"Maybe he stepped out for some groceries."

Kristen could feel Blu's mother giving her a thorough once-over. "It's possible. I found a carton of sour milk in the fridge, three eggs and a six-pack." She patted a brown paper bag on the counter. "That's why I brought my own. I do that from time to time. Have you known my son long?"

"Not too long." There was no way Kristen was going to admit she'd known Blu only two days. This was his mother and she'd found Kristen in her son's bed. In his T-shirt. It was obvious that Mrs. duFray was thinking the worst—though she didn't seem all that upset about it.

"Are you from Algiers, child? I've lived here for over fifty years. Known darn near everyone. Do I know your folks?"

"No. I'm not from around here. I'm from..." Where was she from? "I'm from Florida...St. Petersburg."

"So you're just visiting? Or have you relocated?"

"Visiting."

Kristen scanned the room, looking for the phone. She couldn't wait any longer to call the shelter, and with Blu gone it was the perfect time. When she spied the phone on the wall, she said, "I have to make a call. Do you mind?"

"Not at all, child. You make your call, and I'll get your breakfast on the table. I made eggs. Hope you like them scrambled."

"You didn't need to fuss."

"Nonsense, child. Everyone needs to eat. Except for my son, it seems."

Kristen reached for the phone on the wall and quickly punched in the shelter's number. At the last minute, she took the cordless into the bedroom. "Sister Marian, please," she whispered into the phone once it was picked up.

A moment later the sister was speaking. "This is Sister Marian. How can I help you?"

"This is Kristen."

"Oh, my dear. Are you all right?"

"Yes, I'm fine. And Amanda?"

"She's fine, dear. Missing you, but we're becoming friends. I believe she's beginning to trust me a bit."

"I'm sorry I didn't come back to the room last night, or call sooner. Something happened and… I have a favor to ask. It's really important and if—"

"Ask dear. If it's within my power, I'll be happy to help. It's just such a relief to hear your voice and know you're all right."

Kristen felt tears sting her eyes. "I can't make it back to the shelter today. Maybe not even tomorrow.

Take care of Amanda, please. And if someone comes looking for us— What I mean to say—''

''We've never seen you or know anything about a child. Is that what you wanted me to say?''

''Yes. I know that means—''

''Here at the shelter we don't call it lying, dear. We call it doing the Lord's work. And where are you now, dear? How can I find you if I need to?''

Did she dare tell? Yes, she had to. If there was an emergency Sister Marian needed to be able to reach her. ''I don't want you to get the wrong idea, but I'm staying with the Blu Devil on his boat the *Nightwing.*''

''With the Blu Devil. Oh, my dear, are you sure you know what you're doing? Is he... He hasn't hurt you, has he?''

''No. He's treating me fine,'' Kristen assured her. ''Sister Marian, if you could just watch Amanda for a few days I would be so thankful.''

''It's as good as done. Anything else?''

''The *Nightwing* is moored at the marina in River Bay. Here, I'll give you this number just in case there's an emergency.'' Kristen recited the number. ''I'm making progress, Sister Marian. Staying close to the source is very important right now.''

''The source meaning Blu duFray?''

Kristen hesitated, then finally said, ''Yes. I believe he's the only one who can help.''

''Then do what you must. And I'll do what I do best. I'll storm the heavens with prayer and watch over Amanda.''

Again Kristen had to hold back tears. ''Thank you, Sister Marian. And give my daughter a huge hug and tell her Mommy will be back soon.''

When Kristen returned to the galley, there was a

large bowl of fruit on the table and Rose was dishing up the eggs.

"Sit, child."

She did as Blu's mother suggested, and slid onto the bench that wrapped the table. Rose poured two coffees and, setting one next to Kristen's plate, she eased down on the bench cradling a mug of her own with hands that were used to hard work.

"Can I be blunt?"

Kristen looked up from studying the older woman's hands. "Let me guess. You want to know how old I am."

Rose hesitated, then said, "Yes, that was going to be my question. You look terribly young. Too young to be… Ah, just how old are you?"

Old enough to have a *child* of my own, Kristen wanted to say. Instead, she made a good guess. "I'm twenty-one."

"Really?"

"Yes, really. All my sisters and brothers look really young, too. My mother still doesn't have a gray hair on her head. We just don't age, I guess." Kristen picked up the fork and began to eat, finding it hard to swallow—the lie she'd just told was so huge it had gotten lodged in her throat. "Blu said you own a fish market in town."

"One of them. So, Blu has told you about his family?"

"A little. He mentioned a sister, too."

"Did he now?" Suddenly Blu's mother was making herself more comfortable at the table. "My children are very close. What else did my son tell you?"

Kristen took a sip of her coffee. "I know he owns the duFray Devils, and that he works very hard."

"Yes, very hard. He's a good boy, my Blu."

Kristen stopped eating. Blu's mother had suddenly turned a little somber. "He's been good to me," she heard herself say.

Rose brightened. "He has? Well, that's just wonderful. When he was a youngster he used to sneak onboard the *Demon's Eye* and hide until Carl was too far from shore to turn back. He was a handful, that I can't deny. But always a good boy. Though he did skip school to go fishing. I tell him he's half the reason my hair is gray." She chuckled. "The other reason is raising a daughter with a mind as quick as Margo's."

Kristen liked Rose duFray. She was simple, open and easy to talk to. "Blu's very lucky to have you," she said.

"Oh, I don't know about that."

Blu's mother was dissecting her again. Kristen flushed. "I'm not sleeping with your son, Mrs. duFray. I know what it looks like, but Blu's just letting me stay on his boat for a few days. We're just friends."

Kristen watched as Rose mulled over the information. Then she said, "Finish your breakfast, child. I've got something to show you. I'll bet you'll agree that my son was as handsome growing up as he is now. You do think he's handsome, don't you?"

Before Kristen could answer, Rose was on her feet, tugging her large straw purse off the counter. A moment later she was shoving Kristen's empty plate aside and handing her a purse-size picture album of the Blu Devil.

The Red Lizard was a seedy bar that catered to the weak and desperate. It was also where Blu knew he would find Patch Pollaro. Located on the north side of the French Quarter, the bar's front entrance was littered with idle bodies waiting to call their bookies or their drug suppliers.

Blu shouldered his way through the sorry sight and opened the bar's black door with a red lizard painted on it. It was considered early for a bar to be open, but the Red Lizard never closed. And to prove that Patch Pollaro's open-twenty-four-hours policy was a paying proposition, it was barely ten and there was already a line at the bar.

It had been close to a year since Blu had darkened Patch's front door, and he hadn't left with his boss's blessing.

Inside, he made eye contact with Squeeze, the three-hundred-pound bartender. The man with the bleached-blond crew cut had gotten his name because he wasn't only the Red Lizard's bartender, but the man who *squeezed* the truth out of every potential back room customer before they were allowed to plead their case in front of Patch.

"Had me a feelin' you'd be back." Squeeze grinned. "A hundred dollars a pop, ain't that what you said?" He chuckled. "Good money's hard to walk away from, ah, *mom ami?*"

Blu remained sober, like always, and headed for the office behind the bar. Rapping his knuckles against the all-red door, he waited.

Patch never answered his door with any class, mostly because he had none. He hollered, "What the hell you standing out there for? I'm in here."

Blu opened the door and stepped inside. The minute Patch looked up and saw who had entered his office, his scowl turned into a reckless grin that flashed three gold teeth. "Well, if this isn't my lucky day? I knew you wouldn't be able to stay away. I just knew it."

"Jumping to conclusions gets a man in trouble," Blu drawled.

"No, sleeping with your neighbor's wife gets a man in trouble. This country was founded on speculation and jumpin' the gun."

At sixty-eight, Patch Pollaro wore his gray hair in a ponytail, had a gold ring on every finger, and two in each ear. His love affair with satin vests made him look like a riverboat gambler. The black velvet patch he wore over his left eye added to the overall look, only it wasn't for show—an angry customer had climbed over his desk with a knife and put out Patch's eye a few years back. That was when Squeeze had been installed out front, and Clinton Pollaro's nickname—Patch—had been born.

Blu closed the door behind him and glanced around. Nothing had changed in a year. Patch was still living lean and fast. His office was no more than four stark walls, a cheap metal desk and a huge iron safe. For comfort there was one chair, a cheesy, red-velvet monster with giant armrests—Patch's throne.

Patch's grin widened. "Sure is good to see you, Blu boy."

Because Blu didn't feel the same, he kept silent and crossed the room to stand at the window. For a view, Patch's office overlooked a rancid alley full of ripe garbage and more bodies waiting on a miracle. Deciding the direct approach would be best, he said, "I've come to do a little business with you."

"So this isn't about working for me, it's about needing money?"

As Blu turned from the window, he watched Patch

pull a silver case from his vest pocket, extract a long black cigarette, then slip the case back into his green-satin vest pocket.

"No, I don't need a loan."

Patch lit up, then leaned back on his throne and blew out a stream of smoke. "Well, that's my business, Blu boy, remember? I share my money with the world and then they share their money with me."

"One job," Blu said. "Pick the meanest son of a bitch who owes you the most, and I'll bring him to you on his knees ready to pay up. And in return, you'll make a few phone calls for me and get me some information."

"Information?"

"That's right."

"A rank job for information? That's your deal?"

"The rankest," Blu agreed. "For hard facts."

"Credible information can be costly."

Blu didn't say anything. One job was all he was willing to do. And it was a fair deal.

Patch puffed some more on his cigarette. "You know I always liked you. Damn if I could ever figure out why."

"Because I always got you your money," Blu pointed out.

"That's true. Tell me a little bit about this information. Maybe it's over my head."

"Nothing's over your head." Blu wasn't trying to flatter Patch, just state facts. "I'll have an agreement first, then I'll name-drop."

Grinning again, Patch slid off his big chair, then stepped around his cheap desk. "Now I remember, Blu boy, that's why I always liked you. You were smart. Muscle and guts don't go far in this business if you ain't smart. And you were the smartest badass muscle in the city. Hell, yes, we got a deal, Blu boy. Hell, yes."

Blu nodded, then stated the terms once more, this time ready to drop names. "A rank job, for information on a man named Salvador Maland, and a woman he calls Kristen Harris."

Patch sobered, then finally nodded. "We got a deal, Blu boy."

"Then who do I hit?" Blu asked. "What's the name of the poor slob you want on his knees?"

"Can I have him tonight?" Patch rubbed his hands together like an anxious kid.

"Sure."

"Then I'll see you back here at eight with my cousin, Big Lester. He started out owing me a grand. Now it's up to eight. I've tried to impress upon him that family still has to pay their bills, but..."

What Patch meant to say was that none of his men had been able to bring Lester to his knees. And Blu knew why; Lester worked in the underground pit as a professional fighter. He'd actually killed men in the ring for sport.

"And what about my information?" Blu asked. "When do I get it?"

"If you bring Lester to me tonight, I'll turn my rats loose on the city by nine. We'll have what you want in two, maybe three days."

Patch stuck out his hand. Blu took hold of it and pumped it. Patch was big on handshakes. It's how he ran his operation: a handshake, a Glock in his back pocket, and Squeeze listening at the door.

It was just before noon when Blu boarded the *Nightwing*. As he started down the stairs, he heard his ma's voice. Cursing under his breath, he found Angel perched in a chair with his mother braiding her long blond locks. So engrossed in friendly chatter and looking at pictures, they hadn't even heard him descend the stairs.

Blu lingered in the doorway, one hand on his hip, his shoulder propped against the jamb. His eyebrows rose as he listened to his mother inaccurately detailing an old story he'd just as soon forget.

"Blu was responsible for saving Fern Needle's life," she was saying. "She was so lonely after her husband died. She never had any children, you see. Well, Blu borrowed Grady Fink's cat and gave it to Fern so she would have something to love. It was the sweetest thing. Knowing she was lonely and struggling, well, he—"

"Grady was starving that old Tom cat," Blu interjected. "And I didn't borrow him, I stole him, just like I did his newspaper every Saturday morning just to piss him off."

Rose gasped and spun around. Angel did the same.

Blu, wearing a scowl, stayed where he was. "You got that story twisted, Ma. I didn't give a damn about that cat or old lady Needles. She had an odd smell, and so did that cat. They were perfect for each other."

"How long have you been standing there?" Rose huffed. "You nearly gave me a heart attack, sneaking around like that."

"I don't need to sneak. This is my boat, remember? You done boring Angel?"

"Oh, she wasn't boring me." Kristen piped up.

Blu's gaze shifted to the woman whose voice was beginning to torment him as much as her mouth and brown eyes. Not to mention her little curvy body packaged so perfectly in Lema's sarong. He wanted to ask her if she was all right. If she'd slept okay. He felt his mother's eyes on him and decided to keep his frown in place instead. "Why are you here, Ma?"

"I got a postcard from Margo." She reached for her purse and dug out a card and handed it to him.

Blu took the postcard, eyed the cows on the front, then flipped it over. The message was brief. Margo had met Ry's brother and his mother and father. She was enjoying the trip but missed them both. She and Ry would be back in six or seven days, and if there was time, she'd send another card. Oh, and by the way, these cows looked just like the ones on Ry's brother's ranch.

Blu handed the postcard back to his mother, then glanced at his watch. "You still opening at noon on Tuesdays?"

"Yes."

"Then you're going to be late."

"Oh, dear." Rose snatched up her purse. "I've got to run, child. If you'd be so kind as to drop my pictures by when you're finished, I would—"

Blu shoved away from the doorjamb, bunched up the pictures in his huge hand and dropped them carelessly back into his mother's straw purse. The photo album in Angel's lap followed. "She's done, Ma. Better get going. You wouldn't want customers standing on the street thinking you've forgotten about them."

"I would never forget about my customers," Rose huffed. But as she said the words, she was glancing at her watch, moving through the galley and toward the stairs. "It was nice meeting you," she called. "Come by the store, child. Oh, Blu, I filled the fridge. That milk was sour. Smelled to high heaven."

There was a long silence after his mother left. Blu watched Angel shove back on the chair and fold her hands in her lap. He tried to ignore her baby-soft bare shoulders, and her smooth pretty legs. Better to concentrate on her face, he thought, until his eyes found her mouth and the memory of what she tasted like slammed another heat surge into his groin. It was enough to make him groan. Instead, Blu reminded himself that from here on out there would be no more touching her, and definitely no more kissing her. She'd been hurt, and in the worst way possible. He wasn't going to add to her problems by pawing her with sweating hands and breathing on her as though he were trying to put out a fire.

"Would you like something to eat? Your mother made me eggs for breakfast. I could—"

"I'm not hungry. My mother sometimes gets carried away. Sorry if she made you uncomfortable—"

"She didn't."

"I checked on you before I left. You were sleeping like a log. I thought you might sleep 'til noon."

"I haven't slept that good since I left the island."

"The island? What island is that?"

"I—I didn't mean to—"

"Let it slip?"

"Where I've been living isn't really important."

Blu tried to control his anger. Hell with that, he thought. He had a right to be angry, he was out scrounging information while she was holding back. "You made it sound like Maland lived somewhere close by."

"I never said that."

"You implied it." Blu sauntered forward and dropped down on the couch a few feet away. "What is it, you still don't trust me?"

"I do trust you. I do."

Her words, the conviction behind them, were as much of a surprise as his mother dropping in for a visit. Blu studied her for a moment, then said, "Prove it. You've got a little secret that you've been hiding and I know what it is. If you trust me, you'll share it."

"You know what I've been hiding?"

Blu watched all the color drain from her face. Stretching out in the chair and getting comfortable, he said, "You said you trust me. Here's your chance to prove it."

He'd found out about Amanda. Kristen was glad she was sitting down. He had admitted that he'd followed her to the shelter the other night. Had he gone inside? Had he searched out Sister Marian? So now what? Did she confess, or should she wait to see just how he felt about her having a daughter?

"So where's this island?"

It wasn't what Kristen had expected him to ask. "The island is off the coast of Belize. It's very small. I don't think it even has a name."

She watched Blu kick off his slip-on leather shoes to reveal tanned bare feet. Stretching out, his long toes came within inches of touching her own bare feet. It was strange how intimate bare feet could be, stranger yet was the rising urge Kristen had to slide her toes forward to touch him. But she didn't—this was no time to be thinking about touching the Blu Devil's bare feet. Amanda's safety was in jeopardy.

Kristen dragged the braid over one of her bare shoul-

Play the
"LAS VEGAS"
GAME
GET 3 FREE GIFTS!
FREE GIFTS!
FREE GIFTS!
FREE GIFTS!
TURN THE PAGE TO PLAY!
Details inside!

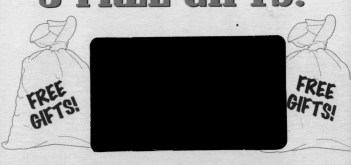

The Silhouette Reader Service™ —Here's how it works:

Accepting your 2 free books and gift places you under no obligation to buy anything. You may keep the books and gift and return the shipping statement marked "cancel." If you do not cancel, about a month later we'll send you 6 additional novels and bill you just $3.80 each in the U.S., or $4.21 each in Canada, plus 25¢ shipping & handling per book and applicable taxes if any.* That's the complete price and — compared to cover prices of $4.50 each in the U.S. and $5.25 each in Canada — it's quite a bargain! You may cancel at any time, but if you choose to continue, every month we'll send you 6 more books, which you may either purchase at the discount price or return to us and cancel your subscription.

*Terms and prices subject to change without notice. Sales tax applicable in N.Y. Canadian residents will be charged applicable provincial taxes and GST.

If offer card is missing write to: Silhouette Reader Service, 3010 Walden Ave., P.O. Box 1867, Buffalo, NY 14240-1867

NO POSTAGE
NECESSARY
IF MAILED
IN THE
UNITED STATES

BUSINESS REPLY MAIL

FIRST-CLASS MAIL PERMIT NO. 717-003 BUFFALO, NY

POSTAGE WILL BE PAID BY ADDRESSEE

SILHOUETTE READER SERVICE
3010 WALDEN AVE
PO BOX 1867
BUFFALO NY 14240-9952

ders. Carefully she said, "I don't know why I didn't tell you about the island."

"Sure you do."

His expression was devoid of any emotion, and Kristen decided Blu duFray was the most serious person she had ever met. He probably hadn't cracked a smile since he was five years old.

"Trust doesn't come easy with you, you said that once. But like I told you, not trusting anyone isn't the answer, *fille.* It's trusting the right someone."

"And as I recall, you said that would be you."

"The biggest mistake you can make now is not leveling with me."

Kristen wished she knew how Blu felt about children. Why didn't he just come out and mention Amanda? Some men felt strongly about fathers being able to keep in touch with their children. What if Blu was one of those men, or what if he simply despised babies?

"Come on, Angel. Tell me about the years you spent with Salvador Maland. Paint me a picture."

Again, what he was asking surprised Kristen. Maybe he was just trying to get her to admit she'd had a child by Salva. Suddenly she felt defensive. "If you know my secret, why don't you fill me in? My memory doesn't work, remember?"

"I'm not asking you about facts before the accident. I'm talking about the island and your life with Maland."

"Can you be more specific?"

Suddenly he sat up, drawing his long legs beneath him. "I want to hear you say it, dammit!"

Kristen held her ground. "I'm not confessing anything," she said stubbornly.

"Just how violent can your boyfriend be, Angel? You've got bruises on your arms. Where else?"

Kristen couldn't hold Blu's gaze a moment longer and she lowered her eyes to her lap. It was almost as if he already knew *where else.* But how could he know *that?* And for what reason had he brought up her bruises? They were talking about Amanda. Weren't they?

She heard him swear, and when she glanced up she saw him drop to his knees and move toward her. Suddenly his hands were shoving up the sarong, and at the same time, spreading her thighs apart. Kristen cried out and tried to squeeze her legs back together, pushing him away at the same time. When she couldn't make him stop, she lunged forward to try to get away, but it only made things worse.

He wrestled her to the floor, and in a matter of seconds he had her pinned down, one of his legs wedged between her legs in a way that opened her wide. "Now," he said a little breathless from their tussle, his forearm resting across her chest to keep her still, "what the hell is that?"

Kristen didn't have to look down to know what he was questioning. How he even knew about the old bruises on her inner thighs was as much a shock as it was a mystery. But the fact was, he did know they were there, and by the look on his face he also knew what had caused them. Dread swept over Kristen and she went limp, all the fight going out of her in a heartbeat. Mortified, she squeezed her eyes shut and let the heat from her embarrassment flood her cheeks. Turning her head as far away as she could, tears filled her eyes.

She heard him swear, this time low and regretfully, she thought. Then suddenly he was off her and pulling her up with him. Kristen kept her face turned away and her body limp as he lifted her into his arms. Then he was on the couch again, cradling her on his lap.

"Dammit, don't cry. Shh. I'm sorry."

Kristen didn't want to cry. She'd already shed too many tears over Salva's repeated cruelty. It had been a horrifying shock that first time, then it had become her dirty little secret she couldn't tell anyone. But as much as she wanted to tell someone, to confess her pain, she didn't want it to be Blu duFray.

"Let me go, please," she whispered.

"No."

She buried her face, and tried to weep as quietly as she could.

"He's never going to hurt you again," he drawled next to her ear. "I promise, *mon ange.* Do you hear me? I promise."

"I didn't want anyone to know," Kristen insisted. "I still don't."

"Your secret is safe with me."

Your secret. It was then that Kristen knew Amanda was still well hidden in the shelter. That the secret Blu had been wanting her to confess all this time had been Salva's abuse.

"How did you find out?" Kristen asked, still unable to meet his gaze.

"Last night... While you were sleeping. I didn't...I didn't do anything to you, so don't worry that I—"

"I'm not worried."

His hand brushed her hair away from her face, then lifted her chin. "The secret goes no further. You trust me, and that's good." Gently he brushed a tear from her cheek. "I have to be gone for a little while tonight. Will you be okay here alone?"

Kristen sat up a little straighter on his lap. "Can't I go with you?"

"No. I want you out of sight. I don't even want you topside. Understand?"

Kristen shivered at the thought of Salva closing in. "I could wear the wig. And I wouldn't be any trouble, I—"

He shook his head. "I'll be back no later than midnight."

She laid her head on his shoulder. "What are you doing this afternoon?"

"At the moment, holding you."

Kristen could feel his gaze on her face. She didn't look up, and instead of climbing off his lap, she curled against Blu like a cat seeking a warm place to take a nap and closed her eyes.

Chapter 9

Big Lester answered his front door wearing red boxers and nothing else. When he learned Blu's intentions, he tipped back his head and laughed so hard by the time he was done, his face was as red as his shorts.

"Thought you'd given up being Patch's ankle biter, boy?"

Blu thought he had, too, and being reminded of it only made his already black mood blacker. "So what do you say, Les, should we head over to the Red Lizard? Both of us walking, or just one of us?"

"You think you're tough enough to take down Lester Batou?" The older man roared out his laughter again. "I don't think so, coonass. No, I don't think the Blu Devil's got it in him no more. Word is, you've turned soft since your sister married that fancy cop."

Blu didn't remember Lester being this tall—six feet, ten inches at least. And he'd put on weight this past year—he had to weigh one hundred pounds over Blu.

"Can't believe everything you hear, Les. Word is you're slowing down, but I'm willing to wait and make that call for myself."

"But you think you're faster, ain't that right, boy?"

Blu shrugged. "You got two choices here, Les. You can either come along and face Patch on your own power, or see just how fast I still am. But one way or the other, we will be paying Patch a visit tonight."

Lester spit a wad of black smear on the porch of his bayou shanty, just missing his already-sticky beard and Blu's booted foot. "Patch tell you we're blood kin?"

"He mentioned it."

"Mangy bastard ain't got no loyalty ta kin."

"Les, you got his eight grand?"

"Maybe I do, and maybe I don't."

"You shook his hand for a grand, right? You know what that means."

"I don't care what the hell it means. He can take that handshake and shove it. You want me down at the Lizard, come on and take me, boy."

Blu let a minute lapse, just in case Lester wanted to rethink his decision. When it didn't happen—no surprise there—he started up the steps. On the porch, he made a quick move to the right, then drove his knee into the giant's groin, countering with a hard left to Lester's protruding gut.

Lester gave a weak grunt, but neither blow rocked him. A second later, he grinned.

And that's when Blu knew it was going to take a little more sweat to bring Lester to his knees than he'd first thought. He had never lost a fight in his life, however, and this time he had a different reason altogether for winning. This time it wasn't about money, or proving he hadn't *gone soft.* This time it was about a promise. He'd never made one of those to anyone before—not a verbal promise anyway. It was enough motivation—that, and remembering how Angel had felt in his arms as she slept in his lap that afternoon.

And so Blu waded in, determined to have Lester Batou on his knees in front of Patch's desk by eight.

Kristen called to check on Amanda after Blu left to see to his business. Sister Marian assured her that everything was fine. She made herself a sandwich from the groceries Rose had left, then fell asleep on the couch.

She woke up with a start some hours later and knew that someone had come aboard the *Nightwing*. She checked the clock and found it was a little after ten. Blu had said he wouldn't be home until midnight so she knew it wasn't him.

She entered the galley and quietly retrieved a frying pan from the cupboard. She fleetingly wished she had the small .22, but she had no idea where Blu had put it—she hadn't seen it for a couple of days.

It was dark in the galley, and as footsteps started down the stairs, Kristen sucked into the shadows and raised the frying pan. A moment later the light came on and Blu was standing at the bottom of the stairs. He looked terrible. "Oh, God! What happened?"

He stared at her, then at the frying pan. "Next time, get the gun. It's in the nightstand drawer." He walked past her then, straight into the bedroom.

"Blu? Your arm...it's..." Unable to stay away, Kristen set down the frying pan and trailed after him. In the doorway, she watched as he pulled a pair of clean jeans from a drawer and disappeared into the head. Uncertain what to do, she simply stayed where she was, wringing her hands and chewing on her lip. She heard the shower start up, and when he came back to the bedroom minutes later, she was still standing in the same spot, wondering and waiting, worried and nervous.

He'd pulled on the clean jeans, but that was it. He'd even neglected to finish buttoning them. In his hand, he carried a large first-aid kit.

The cut on his arm was just above the elbow and wrapped around his arm a good two inches. There was a mark on his neck she hadn't seen when he'd first come down the stairs. From the length and placement it looked as if someone had grabbed his throat and squeezed. It was red and discolored, slightly swollen.

Kristen finally found her legs and came forward. "Here," she took the first-aid kit from him and set it on the nightstand, "let me help you."

"I can do it."

"I'm sure you can, but you don't need to." When she turned, he'd already taken a seat on the bed. "Are you ready to tell me what happened?"

"It's obvious, isn't it? I've been fighting. Someone says or does something I don't like, I take them down. Remember Sam? I lied when I said I didn't enjoy hitting him. I loved every minute of it."

He wasn't making any sense. Kristen shook her head. "Of course you don't love hurting people. I noticed you're limping more than usual. Do you have other injuries?"

"Lester tried to—" He stopped, glared at her.

"Did tonight have something to do with me?"

"Not everything I do these days has to do with you."

His voice was hard, filled with hostility, hostility toward her. Why? "I'm sorry," Kristen said softly. "I didn't mean—"

"I had a life before you showed up in Poke Alley four days ago and pulled that gun on me. There's more to me than you think. Don't be so naive. If I tell you I like hitting people, believe it. And get some backbone. Nobody likes a mouse."

Kristen tried to keep her chin from quivering. She didn't know why Blu was saying such hurtful things, but she had no desire to ask. He was in pain, maybe....

"Are you going to toss a bandage on this or watch me bleed all over the bed?"

Kristen turned to the first-aid kit, opened it, and promptly froze; every bandage size and shape ever invented was inside. Why would he have such an extensive first-aid kit? He just said he liked fighting. Was he telling the truth?

When she didn't move, he glanced at her, then at the first-aid kit. "Haven't you seen bandages before?" He flipped through the sizes, pulled out one that would service the wound on his arm and tore it open.

Sick of his rude and uncalled-for hostility, Kristen snatched the bandage from him and peeled back the protective plastic. As he stuck out his arm, she slapped it on with enough force to make him holler.

"Ouch! Hell, what are you trying to do?"

"I'm practicing getting some backbone," she snapped. "And for an encore I'm out of here."

She spun around to leave, but he reached out and snatched her back. "You can't leave! Don't be a little idiot. You need me to—"

Kristen jerked away from him. "Let's get something straight. I don't need you for anything. I managed to get away from Salva on my own, and I certainly don't *need* another man in my life telling me I'm naive, or how weak I am. When I leave here, I'll—''

He was immediately in her face. ''You're not leaving, dammit! Not until I say it's safe.''

Eyes narrowed, Kristen dodged the bed to stay on her feet as he stalked her. ''Why do you care? You have another life, remember?''

He didn't say anything to that, just stopped and stepped aside. ''Okay, then go, dammit!''

Chin raised, Kristen hesitated only a second before she started for the door. Two steps is as far as she got before he reached out and lifted her off her feet and dropped her onto the bed.

''God, you're naive. Did you really think I would let you walk out of here? You're a sitting duck for this creep.''

''A naive duck with no backbone,'' Kristen snarled.

Suddenly he was smiling. It was a real smile that seemed to surprise him as much as it did Kristen. Her pride still stinging, she sniffed. ''So you really do have teeth. I was beginning to wonder.''

Amusement filled his eyes. ''She's got fangs and claws. Now if I can just teach her how to use them.''

Kristen stared up at him, angry, yet unable to stop admiring his smile. Finally she said, ''You have another cut on your arm. It needs a bandage, too.''

''Are you offering?''

Yes, she was, but she really didn't know why; after all, he had been downright nasty. She stood and shoved him down where she'd been sitting. Once again she glanced at his arm. The cut was on the same arm she'd already bandaged, only not as deep and higher up, slashed lengthwise on his thick, bulging bicep.

Kristen rummaged through the various bandage sizes

until she found the one that would fit the best. When she turned, she caught Blu rubbing his thigh. His eyes were closed, and as he worked the muscle, his face visibly expressed his pain. This time when she applied the bandage, she gently laid the strip over the cut. "I'm sorry for being so rough before."

"I goaded you."

"Yes, you did."

He opened his eyes. "Then it's my turn to say I'm sorry."

He closed his eyes again, then leaned back and flattened out on the bed, again rubbing his thigh.

"What can I do?" Kristen eased onto the bed. "Your leg… You never said what happened."

"No, I didn't."

"And?"

"It's an old wound."

"It can't be too old if it pains you so much."

"Some wounds never heal," he answered, his eyes still closed.

And some just need the right touch, Kristen thought, reminded of how easy it had been for Blu to wipe away her old pain and fear with a single kiss. She reached out and, brushing his hand away, slid her fingers over his thigh. Slowly, gently, she began to knead the muscle the way she had watched him do.

"God, that feels good."

The anger was gone from his voice, and the old Blu, the one she felt safe with, returned. Kristen moved closer, continued to massage his thigh, her fingers enjoying the feel of him, as well as her body.

"Blu?"

"Hmm…"

"Remember last night when you kissed me at Spirit World?"

"I remember."

"You kissed me because you thought I was going to scream?"

"That's right."

Kristen's hand stilled on his thigh. "And that was the only reason?"

She watched him open his eyes and suddenly they were locked in an intense silent stare. When he said nothing, Kristen slowly sat up. Then stood.

"Take it easy now." He sat up, shoved his black hair away from his face. "It was just a way to keep you quiet. You've got nothing to worry about."

A way to keep you quiet. No backbone. Naive. Weakling. It registered, then, what he was really saying. Of course she didn't have anything to worry about. No man was interested in *used merchandise.*

Kristen took a step back. He had a right to feel disgusted by what she had allowed Salva to do to her, that was true enough. She was disgusted herself. Still, the lump in her throat was cutting off her air and making her eyes sting. Oh, God, she didn't want to cry. It would make her look twice as naive. Twice the weakling. And she had actually thought he had enjoyed kissing her.

Kristen blinked fiercely and won the battle. But the Blu Devil was a man who was used to reading between the lines. "What is it? What's wrong? You have no reason to be afraid."

"Nothing's wrong. And I'm not afraid. I'm fine."

"You don't look fine."

Kristen sniffed. "Thanks a lot. You're just full of wonderful words to describe me tonight. Disgusting.

Naive. Now I'm ugly. That's just what every girl wants to—''

''What the hell are you talking about?'' He was really studying her now, his eyes searching. ''Are you going to cry?''

''Over your opinion of me. Ha!'' Kristen wanted to leave with dignity, but instead she bolted out of the room—she'd been such an idiot.

She was up the stairs and almost across the boat deck before she was wrenched off her feet and fused to Blu's hard body.

''Let go!'' Kristen fought as she had never fought before. ''I said, don't touch me you...you oversize...tree.'' She kicked out, swung her fists, forgetting all about his injuries. He grunted in pain, but his arms still banded around her. She slapped his cheek, then bit his shoulder.

He swore when she tried to lift her knee into his groin.

While she still pummeled him, he turned and carried her back down the stairs. She was still screaming, still abusing him as he passed through the galley and made it down the hall to the bedroom. He dumped her on the bed, backtracked and shut the door, then leaned against it.

Kristen scrambled off the bed, her pride wounded, her nostrils flaring. ''I want out of here!''

''Not until I've figured out what the hell just happened.''

His cheek was red where she'd slapped him, and she'd left a faint imprint of her teeth on his left shoulder. Kristen felt ashamed. She'd been crazy to think Blu could be interested in her. After all, she was a woman with no memory and a bruised body that clearly defined her as another man's plaything.

"Listen, I already told you you can trust me. After what Maland did to you I understand your fear. I agree that kissing you at Lema's wasn't the smartest idea. We let… I let it go too far. When I touched you like I did… Well, I know I had no right to do that." He held up a hand, as if he were a Boy Scout swearing an oath. "Don't worry, I don't intend to touch you like that again. I don't enjoy…"

Kristen refused to cry. "I think the word you're looking for is 'whore.' I know what letting a man climb all over me makes me. What men think about women like that."

"What? Hell, that's not what I'm thinking. Where did that come from?" He started toward her. "You've got it all wrong."

"Don't." Kristen shook her head, took another step backward. "Don't come near me. I get the picture."

"No, I don't think you do."

He took two more steps. This time it was Kristen's turn to hold up her hand. "Don't. Don't even think about touching me."

"Oh, I'm going to touch you. That's the one thing you can be sure of, *fille*."

"No!"

"I was keeping my distance for your sake, trying to ease your mind. I didn't want you to think I was helping you for the wrong reason. But what you're thinking now is far worse."

"You said you kissed me to shut me up."

"Okay, I lied." He shrugged. "I gave you the excuse I thought you needed to hear to feel safe."

"I told you I wasn't afraid of you," Kristen argued.

"Meaning what? Exactly what do you want from me?"

Kristen didn't feel confident enough to admit that his kiss had rocked her world. That she had wanted him to kiss her again, to hold her. To do more than just hold her. She fell back on safe words. "I know what I am, and you do, too. A man doesn't want another man's—"

"Don't tell me what I want. It's been hell keeping my hands off you. I've been living with tight jeans for days."

His admission shocked her, then sent her gaze to his crotch. It was true, his jeans were taut in all the right places. A distinct bulge aligned his zipper.

He started toward her again. Kristen backed up until she had put herself in the corner. "Blu..."

"I like my name coming out of that sweet little mouth of yours. I like the way you run your tongue over your bottom lip afterward." He took two more steps and rocked forward, sniffed. "I like how you smell, too. Like sweet grass and lemon."

Kristen couldn't move, couldn't help wondering what he would do next. She wasn't fool enough to believe that a night spent in Blu's arms would change everything, but she knew for certain that if there was a man on this earth who could cleanse her body and her soul it was Blu duFray.

He reached out and tangled a finger around a long strand of her hair. There was a deep sigh, a rush of air. Kristen was holding her breath so she knew the sigh was his. His eyes roamed her face with a galvanized stare that made her shiver. Again she knew he was trying to read her. Well, she was trying to read him, too. And *that look,* coupled with his body language was making things very clear—the Blu Devil was going to do more than kiss her before the night was over.

So there was no mistake what he read in her eyes, Kristen rested her hands on Blu's bare chest, then, as she parted her lips, she slid her hands upward and wrapped her arms around his neck.

Salvador Maland found his missing sailboat in the coastal village of Punta Gorda. The last stop before the Guatemalan border, the primitive, edge-of-the-world outpost was the last place he had expected to find his expensive sailboat.

He'd spent days searching for Kristen and with each one that passed, his temper slipped a notch. Daily he barked out orders to his men, and at night he paced the deck of his sixty-foot luxury yacht with a military stride that warned his crew his mind was in a very dark place.

Dressed in a black silk jacket and pants, his gold jewelry twinkling in the sunlight, Salva now faced the fisherman whose dock he'd found his missing sailboat tied to. "Your name, old man?"

"Carlos Sancho," answered the stocky fisherman.

"How did you get my boat?" Salva demanded. "And how long have you had it?"

"Your boat?" The man's eyes widened and, after nervously sizing up Salva, his gaze traveled to the six bald-headed men who flanked him. "Dis boat was given to me, *señor*. I git it as a geeft two days ago."

"From who?"

Carlos started to sweat and Salva smiled for the first time in days. It was arousing as hell to witness someone else's fear. "I said, who gave you my boat, old man?"

"I don't know his name, *señor.*"

Two of Salva's men broke away from the line and advanced on the fisherman. The old man's fear took flight and he backed up into the clear water of the Caribbean. "I—I speak the truth, *amigos.* An American jus' come and say, 'Do you want a geeft?' The boat *es* very nice geeft. I say, '*Sí,* thank you,' and he give me the boat."

"What did he look like, the American?"

"Yellow hair, nice shirt. Gold watch."

"Was he alone?"

"Sí."

"You're sure there was no one with him?"

"No one."

"Then what happened?"

"He hired Raphael to fly him north."

Salva sent two of his men to locate Raphael, then motioned to the two standing beside Carlos to take the fisherman aboard his yacht. If the man had anything else he was purposely leaving out, they would know it within the hour. If he didn't… Well, either way, Salva always tied up loose ends.

Back on his yacht, standing at the railing, Salva gave instructions that the stolen sailboat was to be sailed back to his island. A moment later, his cell phone rang. "Yes, Mother?"

"Darling, we've completed the search as you requested. Every room in the house has been taken apart and put back together."

"And did you find anything out of place or missing?"

There was a long pause, then Miandera said, "A gun from your collection in your private office is missing. A small .22, and…"

"Get on with it, Mother! I don't need the dramatics!" Salva was having trouble breathing.

"Amanda's baby album, darling. It's gone, as well."

Salva nearly choked. He leaned into the railing and gripped the iron to keep his balance. Finally, when he was able to speak, he said, "Then you were right, Mother. Kristen plotted her escape and willfully left me."

"Yes, darling." Miandera sighed, and Salva knew his mother was smiling. "I'm sorry, darling. I can't think of anything worse she could do to you than this."

Salva couldn't, either. But then he had no idea that at that very moment his addiction—the woman who had become his entire reason for living—was only seconds away from giving her body to his enemy.

Chapter 10

They'd been kissing for a long five minutes. Blu was trying to go slow and keep it easy. Slow and easy was what Angel needed. But he was on fire and he wasn't so sure that he could continue to hold back.

He leaned in and kissed her once more. He hadn't been with a woman in a while, never with someone like Angel. He steered clear of the young ones, and always the innocent—the dirt on his hands had always made him feel undeserving of something nice. Something clean and good.

And Angel was all that. She may not be a virgin, but she was an innocent just the same. An innocent victim who had gotten caught in someone else's madness.

Blu inched closer, allowed his bare chest to brush her breasts. She arched up slightly, her nipples already hard beneath the sarong. He kissed her again, sucked on her lower lip. He could tell by the way she kissed him back that she had never been where he wanted to take her. Where they were headed.

She was trapped against the wall, but there was no fear in her eyes. Still, he pulled her into the middle of the room and reversed their positions. Sure that Maland's violence still haunted her, he was determined to wipe that horror from her mind.

"What are you doing?" she whispered against his mouth.

"It's not too late to shut me down, Angel. It's never too late. Just say the word and—"

She slid her hands up his bare chest, then reversed the motion and sent them downward. When her tiny fingers curled into the waistband of his jeans, Blu felt his groin swell and pulse. "You can stop now?" She dragged her eyes from his aroused condition to look up at him.

"If I have to," Blu promised.

She smiled up at him. "And that's why I'm not afraid." She leaned in and kissed his chest, brushed her lips over his nipples. Her fingers found his zipper and slid it downward.

Blu had foregone shorts after he'd showered. Naked inside his jeans, his body reacted to being freed, and he groaned as open air touched him. A second later it was her hand that was touching him. He jerked hard, then groaned out loud as his intentions to go slow were suddenly on shifting sand. He closed his eyes and rested his head against the wall, trying to formulate some kind of new plan to keep from losing control and knocking her to his bed and driving into her hard and fast.

"I should take this off, yes?"

Blu opened his eyes, saw that she was fingering the

button that held the sarong in place. He watched her slide the button free, saw the sarong drift to the wooden floor.

Blu nearly swallowed his tongue.

She was completely naked beneath the sarong. He guessed he knew that already, recalling her nude-colored panties hanging in the bathroom on the towel bar. She must have washed them in the sink earlier in the evening and hung them up to dry.

He moaned at the sight of her perfection, then moaned again when she crushed her hot little breasts against his stomach. Seconds later she was on her tip-toes, looking for another gentle kiss.

Blu didn't know how many more of those he had left in him—she was pushing all the right buttons, sending his blood on a mad race in all directions of his body. He wrapped his arms around her, then ran his fingers up her satin-smooth back. Pulling her close, he gyrated his hips against her softness. When she didn't resist, he knew she had just sent him another signal.

"I'm going to lose these," he said, setting her away from him. He sent his jeans to the floor to join her sarong. A half minute later he had her laid out in the middle of his bed. "It's never too late," he drawled as he kissed her lips. Keeping his eyes locked with hers, he placed his hand on her stomach, then began to move it downward, weaving his fingers through the silky blond V between her thighs.

"Make love to me, Blu. Make all the bad go away."

He kissed her again, then feasted on her neck, her collarbone. Finding her breasts, his tongue licked, then sucked.

"Blu..."

"More?"

"Yes. Oh, yes."

He took his time, savored her taste, put to memory her little panting gasps of pleasure. He worshipped her flat stomach with his lips, then his tongue. Headed for the downy curls between her legs, he heard her breath catch, whoosh out. She arched her hips.

"It'll be good, *mon ange*. I promise," he murmured against her flesh, hoping he could deliver on that vow.

"I trust you," she sighed, as if she understood his concern.

Her voice sounded faraway, but there was no mistaking her unmasked desire or the truth in her words. Blu moved back to kiss her lips and taste her sweet breath once more. He wanted to be able to give her what she needed. To give back what Maland had stolen from her.

He started a slow descent again, kissing his way down her body, taking his time to gently touch her, all of her. Her legs were so beautiful, her tiny feet and ankles so delicate as they tangled around him.

He found the bruises on the inside of her thighs and kissed them tenderly with a whisper-soft touch that was more breath than anything else. It was at that moment she became completely his. Overwhelmed by the way she gave herself over to him, Blu ran his tongue slowly over her pulsing flesh, opening her a little at a time with each focused stroke of his tongue. Her hands found his hair, and she bent her knees slightly and pulled up her legs, opening wider so he could send his tongue deeper. Her anxious moans and her sudden urgent twisting on the bed, warned him that he was nearly sending her into a climax.

He backed off, withdrew his tongue, wanting to drag it out, to savor her.

I trust you. I trust you.

On his knees, Blu tugged her up. Rolling onto his back, he set her astride him. She looked beautiful sitting on him, her small firm breasts exposed to his eyes, her fairy-tale hair teasing his hips and chest.

Make love to me, Blu… I trust you. I trust you.

She arched her back, then lifted her hips and slid herself against his hot sex. The friction jerked Blu upward into a sitting position, splintering his resolve. In a husky voice he said, "I thought you might need to go slow."

"Because I've been hurt?" She was looking straight at him, demanding an honest answer.

Blu gave it to her. "No, because you're very small."

His blunt answer wasn't the one she'd expected, he could see it in her eyes. "And you don't want to hurt me?"

"I don't ever want to hurt you," Blu whispered.

Her smile faded, and she was suddenly very aware of her naked breasts visible to his inspection. "I know I'm small in other places, too. The woman on the cover of that *Playboy*—"

"Shh." Blu pulled her close and kissed each small breast. "Everything is beautiful. So beautiful." He moaned as his callused thumbs began to play with her nipples. The look on her face told him she'd felt his growing need on the move. He said, "*Oui,* that was…Harvey. When he likes someone a lot, he starts showing off and acting up."

"Up? Yes, that's where I think he's headed."

Her teasing both surprised and delighted Blu. It relaxed him, brought him down to earth a little. She was so damn sweet, so overwhelmingly beautiful and she *trusted him.*

Before things got out of hand, he pulled open the nightstand drawer and retrieved a condom and slipped it on. "This might make it easier for you," he said, explaining further, "sitting astride me." He shifted his body and slowly started pushing his way into her. "Don't close your eyes, Angel. Stay with me."

Blu was halfway home when passion began to flush her face. Clinging to him now, her arms gripped his shoulders as desire stole her breath. He watched her sugar-sweet brown eyes fill with wonder, felt her quiver as her tight sheath convulsed around the last of his length.

Blu wanted to thrust hard and fast into her, but he checked his desire as best he could, rewarded when Angel's passion drove her upward, then downward on his lap. He moaned loudly, gripped her waist to steady her. "Keep your eyes open, Angel. We're going to take a ride, and you're going to do the driving, remember? It can be as wild and as fast as you want to go, or as slow and careful as you need it to be. Either way, I guarantee we'll get where we're going."

Trusting him, ready to drive, she took his mouth with eager abandon and began to move on him. Blu savored the feel of her, the kill-me friction and the explosive heat that was steadily building. He wanted her any way he could have her. Would have been satisfied with whatever choice she made. Fast, slow. Careful. Wild. But he'd made one mistake—Angel was perfection, and good ol' Harvey, having never tasted perfection in his life, turned up the heat and charged forward.

Blu heard her gasp, then moan in pleasure as he spilled into her. His climax sent her over the edge hard and fast. Reaching for her own euphoria, she clung to him, rode him hard. Eyes locked on his, she kept moving, leading him. Driving him.

He felt her let go, watched her face.

When her soft, satisfied cries had ended and her damp body had grown still, Blu kissed her gently, then pulled her close. As they melted back to earth, he stretched out on the bed with her still on top of him, not ready to give up the feel of her skin against his. She was still looking at him. He stared back. The next best thing to feeling Angel's release while he was inside her, he decided, was holding her, her eyes clearly telling him that he'd been responsible for something *new,* something that she had never experienced before.

Well, that made two of them, Blu thought, cradling her against his chest as a strange kind of peace warmed his insides.

He reminded himself not to lose his head. Right now what Angel needed most was not a man blinded by emotions, but a man who knew what was lurking in the shadows. And every instinct Blu owned told him that Salvador Maland was in the shadows, waiting for Angel to make a mistake. She was perfection, an addiction few men would be able to overcome. And a powerful man, with a sick mind, who enjoyed hurting young girls, would see no reason why he should have to.

Kristen felt Blu shudder and she curled against him, burying her face in the soft hair on his hard chest.

"Then you're awake?"

"I'm awake." She squirmed to get closer, but he held her off, kept his lower body just out of reach. Never before had Kristen experienced anything so warm and wonderful as the safe feeling that Blu created when he was inside her. The act could have frightened her, should have after what she'd endured with Salva. But nothing about Blu duFray frightened her, not his size, not his powerful hands, not his devil's reputation. Nothing.

And she'd been right to believe that he would wash away all the pain and ugliness. It was gone, replaced by so much love for this man that Kristen felt as if her heart would burst. Yes, she loved Blu duFray. Loved him with a fierce need that went bone-deep.

"Please..." She found his hips and pulled him to her. "I need to feel you inside me. I want heaven again, Blu. Please."

"Heaven, is it?"

The light rumble of laughter that came from deep inside his chest made Kristen pull back to search out his face. It was the middle of the night and a single candle burned on the nightstand. His face was in shadow, but she could see his dark, beautiful eyes, see his relaxed features. See that he was smiling. "Are you making fun of me, Blu duFray?"

He kissed her. "No. I've just never heard it called that before."

"And what do you call it?"

He arched a brow and grinned down at her.

"Never mind. I can only imagine what kind of names men would call what we just did. I still think heaven is the perfect word for it."

He rolled her onto her back and slowly sank into her, carefully, gently. "Then here, my little angel, have some heaven. I'm ready for another spiritual experience if you are."

It was the first time Kristen had ever heard him tease.

"It's amazing," she teased back, "the *Devil* smiles and make jokes on occasion. I'm learning all kinds of things tonight."

He moved inside her. Kissed her.

Kristen kissed him back. "Do you always make love this way? I mean, I know I'm not suppose to ask that kind of question, but..."

His gaze sharpened, his hips stilled. "I don't know what you're asking. What way is 'this way'?"

"Is Blu duFray's lovemaking always about giving?" His smile widened, and it was so beautiful Kristen nearly cried.

"Do I look like a starving man?"

"No."

"When you give, you get. Ever hear that?"

Kristen giggled. "Yes."

"Then should I reach for a condom, or do you want to slap me down and go back to sleep?"

Kristen shoved Blu onto his back, and sat up. Her gaze traveled down his impossibly hard stomach to where his arousal pulsed hot and hard. Slowly she reached down and wrapped her hand around his length. "I'm curious about something. Do you mind?" She slid her hand upward, then down to the base of him and watched him grow in her hand.

"*Bon Dieu!* A curious *angel,* interested in a man's *heaven.*"

Kristen kissed his stomach, moved her hand slowly back up. She heard him groan and brought her gaze to his face. His eyes were closed, but he was breathing faster.

"*Mais* yeah. That's good. Ah...that, too."

* * *

Blu heard footsteps overhead. Without waking Angel, he slipped from the bed, snared his jeans off the floor, and was out the door quickly.

On deck, in the early-morning sunshine, Blu studied the short, round woman as she wiggled and squirmed to lower her feet to the deck. She was dressed in black, everything from head to toe was black.

Arms crossed over his bare chest, he gave her a second to catch her breath, then said, "You come to rob me, Sister Marian?"

"Ekeee—" The nun jumped a foot off the deck and spun around so quickly she nearly lost her balance and landed on her backside. Eyes wide, she staggered to gain her balance, at the same time she stared at Blu's half-naked body. "Oh, my. Oh, dear. Is she… Is she—"

"Alive. *Oui,* she's here, and alive," he assured. "You got a reason for setting foot on my boat?"

Sister Marian straightened her shoulders and added a half inch to her five-foot frame. "As a matter of fact, I do. This might seem a bit bold, but have you finally decided to accept your responsibilities? You've had plenty of time to decide."

"To decide what?"

"There's nothing wrong with enjoying the fruit as long as you both know that a permanent arrangement must be made for the little one's sake. You agree, don't you?"

"The little one? And just what kind of permanent arrangement must be made?" Blu asked, completely confused at this point.

"Oh, my. She hasn't gotten that far yet. Oh, dear. I believe I've come a bit too early."

"Too early for what?"

Blu's annoyance was showing. He saw the nun

glance toward the dock as if she were contemplating making a run for it. He shook his head. "I wouldn't try it. I don't have any problem with tumbling you."

"Oh, dear. You are a rascal, aren't you?"

"That's me," Blu agreed. "Too early for what? Finish what you started."

The nun crossed herself, then clutched her hands together and whispered something that sounded like a prayer. A moment later she said, "I brought your child. I thought by now you'd be anxious to see her."

For fear of choking, Blu cleared his throat.

"I'll tell you what I think," the nun rushed on. "I think Kristen could do a whole lot better than someone who goes by the name of Blu Devil—" she crossed herself again "—but she seems to think you're worth the trouble. I could be swayed into believing it, if you were to accept that precious child as yours. A good father is what she needs."

Blu's heart started to pound. "I'm nobody's father, sister. You're confused."

"Don't tell me you're going to deny she's yours? Deny them both a home?"

The older woman flushed pink, then went through the motion of crossing herself again. Blu was ready to tie her hands together.

"I was afraid that something like this would happen. Some men lust after only the fruit and nothing more. Oh, dear. Yes, this is exactly what I was afraid of. I must speak to Kristen, and convince her that all is not lost."

She started toward the stairs. Blu gripped the nun's shoulder and stopped her. A moment later he was steering her to the leather bench at the stern. "Sit down."

Eyes wide, Sister Marian plopped onto the bench as

if her knees had suddenly given out. "If you insist, Mr. duFray. Or do you prefer Blu Devil? I must say it's not that I mind the word devil, but for the child's sake—"

"For the child's sake I think you need to start at the beginning. Let's go back to the first day you met Angel."

"Angel? Oh, you mean Kristen. Yes, of course. Well...let's see. I believe it was maybe seven or eight days ago that she and Amanda showed up at the shelter. She told me she was looking for her father, and that she and the little one needed a place to stay. She said that her father left her and her mother years ago and she'd finally tracked him to Algiers. She mentioned you might know him. Well..." Sister Marian, sniffed. "I knew the story was false right from the beginning. It didn't take an Einstein to figure out what she wasn't saying."

"And that was?" Blu probed.

"Well, that she and you... That you...that you're Amanda's father. Shame on you for stealing that young girl's innocence, by the way." The nun crossed herself. "And with your reputation, no less. Have you ever heard of protection, dear boy? Well, obviously not." She sat silent a minute, perspiration forming on her face. She fanned herself a bit. Finally she said, "Now, are you, or are you not going to accept your child and do right by our dear Kristen?"

Blu couldn't believe that if Kristen had a child, she wouldn't have told him. "I have no child, Sister Marian. This kid can't be mine."

"Amanda, her name is Amanda. And she's a beautiful child. Did I mention, well mannered? She won't eat much. She's a miniature of her mama. Delightful child."

A miniature of her mama. That, Blu couldn't deny, piqued his curiosity. He rubbed his jaw, then paced to the railing. "Where is...Amanda?"

"My brother, he's... Tiny, you can come out now."

Blu watched as the Hulk suddenly appeared on the dock, carrying a little blond girl that couldn't be more than two or three. What the hell was going on? he wondered. This was the same guy who'd been chasing after Angel the night she'd run from Cruger's.

"You said he's your brother?" Blu asked.

"Yes. Tiny's my younger brother."

Blu faced the Hulk. "Weren't you the one chasing after Angel the other night?"

Tiny looked embarrassed. "I wasn't chasing her, I was guarding her. But she took off and I lost her. I was watching out for her—at least, I was trying to."

"That's true," Sister Marian confirmed, standing and coming forward. "I sent Tiny out to be Kristen's guardian angel that night. She kept insisting she had to go out at night. I told her how dangerous Algiers is after dark. I was afraid for her safety, so I sent Tiny to protect her."

Blu digested the nun's explanation and decided she was telling the truth. The man's bald head had to be just a bizarre coincidence. Yeah, he could buy that.

He watched as Sister Marian reached out and took Amanda from her brother. The big man stayed on the dock, with a black backpack slung on his shoulder.

The minute Blu took a good look at the baby, he knew she was Angel's child. The sister was right, Amanda was a miniature version of her mother. A mix of unexpected emotions surfaced, emotions Blu wasn't expecting. He'd never taken an interest in kids, but then, last year he'd found himself in the middle of protecting six scared kids who had needed someone to care just a little. He'd been struck by their eyes, though he hadn't admitted that to anyone. The same feeling had caught him unaware a few days ago when he had faced Angel's save-me brown eyes in Poke Alley.

And it was happening again, Blu realized as he stared into a pair of small shy brown eyes that were studying him intently.

The idea that Kristen had given Maland a child should have sickened Blu. But he knew what she'd gone through for three years, and he understood her pain. What hurt most was that she hadn't trusted him enough to tell him about her child.

He turned away from the nun and looked out over the water. The sun was growing stronger, promising another hot, sultry day. The air was barely moving.

"You can't mean to turn your back on the child." The nun had come up behind him. "You called Kristen 'Angel.' You must have some feelings for her to give her such a beautiful name."

Blu didn't answer. He was too busy considering Salvador Maland's state of mind at the moment. Experience told him that if a man had been betrayed and made to look like a fool, it made him a very dangerous man. But what if the man was already dangerous? Angel hadn't only made a fool out of Maland and cut him by leaving him, but she'd thrown salt in the open wound by stealing his child.

Bon Dieu! Blu thought. How was he going to keep her safe when she kept hiding pieces of her life from him? It made him nervous wondering what the hell was coming next.

With surprising strength, the nun grabbed Blu's arm and pulled him around to face her. "I know this must be a surprise, but you certainly knew the risks. Accepting this child is the most honorable thing you can do right now. So here—" the nun shoved Amanda into Blu's arms "—meet your daughter." She turned to her brother. "Do you have the bag, Tiny?"

"Right here."

Blu held Amanda out in front of him at arm's length as the nun hustled to retrieve the black bag Tiny dropped onto the deck. Her little eyes, Blu noted, had grown huge and her bottom lip started to quiver. Her little legs dangled from beneath a soft pink dress. "Oh, hell, can't you see I scare her? Take her back."

The nun spun around, her skirt swinging wide. "She'll warm up to you, just give her a smile. You can smile, can't you? Here, if you hold her like this, she'll like it better."

The nun set down the pack, then demonstrated the proper way to hold Amanda. After which she gave her back to Blu. "Now you do it."

Blu bent his arm and brought Amanda close. She was still staring at him with wary eyes, her lower lip extended to the max in a full pout. He stared at her mouth. It was Kristen's mouth, dainty and sweet. "Listen. She's not—" Blu stopped himself from denouncing the child. It didn't really matter who the father was. She was Kristen's, and she belonged with her mother, not with these strangers, and certainly not with Maland.

Sister Marian pointed to the small black backpack. "That was all she came with. That and the child. If you decide to cast them out, tell Kristen she's welcome back at the shelter. Tell her I'm sorry for not waiting another day. I thought I was helping."

Blu watched as the nun climbed out of the boat with her brother's help. On the dock, she turned back. "I hope you realize just how lucky you are, Blu duFray. You have a beautiful family. Do right by them and God's goodness will shine down on you."

And that was it. Sister Marian and Tiny disappeared, and Blu was left holding the Miniature. He studied her again as she studied him. Finally he said, "You hungry?"

She shook her head, then reached for Blu's hair and pulled.

"Ouch!"

Her lip went out a little farther, and she lowered her head.

Blu tugged her chin up, then found himself smiling. A second later he winked.

"I miss Mommeee," she whispered.

Blu could smell her sweet breath. She was so small, so vulnerable. "I have a surprise for you."

She looked up. "S'prize?"

"If you promise not to wake Mommy, I'll show you where she is."

Her little eyes lit up and she thrust forward and wrapped her arms tightly around his neck. Next to his ear, she whispered, "I pomiss."

Blu felt her fingers in his hair again, but this time she didn't pull. She seemed fascinated by the fact that he had something growing on his head. Knowing why that was, he started down the stairs.

Chapter 11

Kristen was dreaming. Drugged by her sweet daughter's birdlike voice, she rolled onto her side and snuggled with her dream.

"Dis time, I feed Da."

"Wait. Over here, my mouth is over here. Oh, hell, you've got it in your hair. Mine, too. Let me help."

"Da has hair, too."

"Yes, I have hair, too."

Kristen sighed, wondering how Blu had gotten into her dream. Smiling, she decided she knew how—he was the most marvelous man on earth. And she loved him—loved him with all her heart.

"Let's wash you up before Mommy sees you like this."

"Otay."

Kristen opened her eyes slowly. Stretching, her mind began to surface from the dream cloud she'd been riding. She could hear Blu in the galley. Hear Amanda, too. *Amanda?*

''Me wash Da's face.''

Kristen frowned. Listened.

''All right. But after I wash yours.''

''After Da washes meeeee.''

''That's right. Now hold still. No, don't do that. You'll fall. Sit!''

''Da, mad?''

''No, I'm not mad. I just don't want you falling off the counter.''

Kristen sat up quickly and climbed out of bed. Amanda was at the shelter with Sister Marian. She couldn't be—

''Hold still. Let's see if I can get some of this out of your hair.''

Eyes wide, Kristen scanned the floor for her sarong, grabbed it, and slipped it on. She came out of the bedroom on the run, then froze—she could see Amanda was sitting on the counter in the galley and she was...she was washing Blu's face.

He was wearing jeans, and his chest was bare. So were his feet. Amanda had on her only dress, which was now stained with something that resembled egg yolk.

Amanda glanced up. ''See, Mommeee. Me wash Da.''

Kristen watched her daughter dip a washcloth into the sink, then, barely squeezing it out, thrust it at Blu's face and scrub wildly. Giggling, her animated little legs kicked out with excitement and nearly clipped Blu in the groin. He deftly swung his hip, and she missed him by a scant inch.

Slowly he turned, water dripping off his chin and nose. Their eyes met. Locked.

"Oh, God. I—I was going to... When the time was... I was afraid you wouldn't..." Kristen found her legs and she moved forward. Shoving her long hair behind her, she scooped Amanda off the counter and pulled her close. Kissing her daughter's cheek, she whispered, "Mommy missed you. I'm sorry I was away so long, sweetheart."

She turned her back on Blu because she needed some time to pull herself together. When she could still feel his eyes on her, she hurried back into the bedroom and closed the door. She felt as if she had run a race. As if her legs were going to collapse. She sank onto the bed, hugging Amanda. For now she wasn't going to think about Blu and what she had to tell him once she faced him. Right now she was going to focus all her attention on Amanda. It had been too long since she had held her precious baby and cuddled with her. Amanda must have thought so, too, because she was clinging.

An hour later Kristen propped a pillow next to Amanda's sleeping little body and went in search of Blu. She found him on the couch, his long legs sprawled out in front of him. His eyes were closed and, for a moment, she thought he was sleeping.

She was about to turn and leave when he said, "Sit down."

Kristen did as he asked, taking the chair opposite him. His eyes flicked open and he studied her for a long moment.

"She's napping," Kristen explained, not knowing what else to say.

His gaze shifted, drifted over her body. It reminded

Kristen of what they had done only a few hours ago. "Blu... Blu, I'm sorry. I know I should have told you about her. I should have told you days ago, but—"

"But you couldn't trust me."

Kristen hung her head. "I trust you. I just...I just wasn't so sure how you would react to a small child."

He sat up, leaned forward. "What did you think I would do if you told me? Drowned her like an unwanted puppy?"

"No!"

"Did you think I'd walk away from helping you?"

Kristen looked at him. "I was scared, all right? I wasn't thinking. How did she get here? Did—"

"Sister Marian wanted me to tell you that if I threw you and *my* daughter out, you could return to the shelter."

"Your daughter?"

"She said she knew I was Mandy's father, and that I should accept the responsibility."

Kristen's cheeks flamed. "I didn't tell her you were Amanda's father. But I did lie so that she would let me stay at the shelter."

"She told me what you said, and that she'd known it was a lie from the beginning. She said she put two and two together and decided I had abandoned you and *my* daughter a few years ago."

"She misunderstood."

"Do I know the whole truth now? Everything?"

The question had Kristen wringing her hands. All she wanted to do was to go to Blu and curl up in his strong arms. But he wouldn't want anything to do with her once he knew *everything*. Did she have a choice, though? She could lie again and tell him that she had no more secrets, but...

She stood, turned her back and wrestled with her decision. A moment later his hand weighed heavy on her shoulder. She hadn't even heard him come up behind her. "What else, Angel? What's so bad that you can't tell me? Can't even look at me?"

Kristen felt his hand move from her shoulder and, with easy familiarity, wrap around her waist. A little rougher than she expected, he pulled her back against him. Then his heat was surrounding her and last night's memories flooded her senses. She squeezed her eyes shut, wanting to remember, knowing she had no right to love Blu duFray, to want him this badly.

He bent his head, whispered, "I'll help you no matter what. Is that what you're waiting to hear? I'll see you safe, that I promise. Mandy, too. Nothing you can say will make me walk away."

"Are you so sure?" Kristen turned in his arms and gazed up at him. "What if I told you I was married? That I'm Salvador Maland's wife?"

When Kristen had first awakened and found herself on Salva's island with no memory, she had been frantic to remember her past. She'd tried so hard that daily she had made herself sick. So sick, she'd gone to bed with severe headaches. As the weeks passed without remembering anything, she'd decided to accept what she couldn't change and endure her life.

Then Amanda had been born and it was her daughter who had kept Kristen alive, enduring Salva and his cruelty for the sake of her child. Once more Kristen realized that it was Amanda who was keeping her on her feet, keeping her from sinking into a pile of self-pity.

Yes, Blu had walked out, as she'd known he would.

And she was hurting. But she'd been hurt before. It wasn't fatal. Only this time the hurt cut more deeply than ever before because she was in love for the first time in her life. Even without her memory, she knew that Blu duFray was the right man—the only man—she would ever love.

Going back to the shelter was out. After talking to Sister Marian on the telephone, Kristen refused to burden her further. She had been both surprised and relieved to learn that the Hulk wasn't Salva's man, but Sister Marian's younger brother who had been sent to keep her safe on the streets of Algiers after dark.

She didn't have much money, and now she had less since she'd bought a bus ticket—she would be leaving town tomorrow night. But until then she needed a place to stay, and with no money, she was standing outside duFray Fish in the hope that Rose duFray would allow her to spend the rest of the afternoon and one night under her roof.

With Amanda on her hip, Kristen pushed open the door and stepped inside the small shop. She didn't feel all that comfortable asking Blu's mother for such a huge favor, but Rose had been so nice to her the other day that she was hopeful.

Kristen found the clean little market packed with customers. She let the door slam shut behind her, and immediately wished she had waited until closing time to speak to Rose—six people stood in line at the checkout counter.

She glanced around and discovered every kind of fish you could imagine displayed on ice. There was everything from seabass to blue-fin tuna to Grouper, shrimp and oysters.

There was a corner of the shop dedicated to various

spices and sauces, boxed batters and oils. But for the most part the fish market was just that—the most complete fresh-fish outlet on the wharf.

Amanda was pointing, and wanting to get down. With so many people wall-to-wall, Kristen told her no. A line at the cashier had now stalled—the woman paying had suddenly decided to discuss spices with Blu's mother. As Rose came around the counter, she spotted Kristen and her face brightened. On her way to the spices, she stopped and said, "It's good to see you, child." She scooped Amanda into her arms, then pointed to the cash register. "Could you run the register for a little while? Today is a madhouse and my worker called in sick. This must be Mandy."

"Amanda."

"Yes. Blu called looking for you and your daughter. But we'll talk about that later. I'll keep her with me, and you run the register."

Kristen hesitated, then nodded. Amanda was already interested in the bun at the back of Rose's head, and the gold clip keeping it in place.

For the next hour Kristen rang up the purchases behind the counter as Rose pointed and recommended to her loyal customers the best catches of the day. When the crowd began to thin, Rose appeared with a sleeping Amanda on her shoulder. "She finally gave up the fight," she whispered, rubbing Amanda's back. "Why don't you take her up the back steps and put her down? Blu's and Margo's old room is right off the kitchen. There's still two beds in there. You can't miss it. Make yourself comfortable. Make some tea or coffee. If you're hungry—"

"I'm fine," Kristen assured her, taking Amanda from Rose. "Thank you."

She took the stairs and opened the door. Rose duFray lived in a spotless three-room flat that was warm and cozy. The furniture was old, but well cared for, and there were fresh flowers on the small kitchen table.

Kristen walked through the narrow kitchen and straight into the bedroom Rose had mentioned—the room Blu had shared with his sister. Like the rest of the house, it was small, barely large enough for two twin beds. A tall, narrow dresser fit tightly into one corner, in the other was a small table with a picture of Blu and a dark-haired girl who looked a lot like him. It had to be his sister, Margo, Kristen decided.

She eyed the two beds, then eased Amanda off her shoulder and laid her on the one with the fishing motif bedspread—the other spread was peach floral. There was no doubt this was Blu's bed, she decided, the one with the boats and the fish scattered every-which-way.

Feeling a tangle of emotions, she curled up beside Amanda. Rose had said that Blu had called, looking for her. Kristen didn't know how she felt about that. One thing she knew for sure—she should never have lied to him. She regretted that more than she could say, but she would never regret sleeping with him no matter how bad that made her seem. She knew now, married or not, she had never loved Salva, not even before she'd lost her memory. He might be her husband, but not in the real sense of the word. In her heart, she was married to Blu duFray. He may not feel the same way, in fact, she was sure he didn't. But she would always believe she'd done the right thing by giving herself to him. He had mended her broken heart and healed her soul. And that, she truly believed, had been a gift from God.

She realized now that from the moment she had laid

eyes on Blu in Salva's office that she had been hypnotized by him in some way. As crazy as that sounded, she had gotten shivers looking at him, then a heat had settled in her stomach. At the time she'd thought it was simply another dose of fear—after all, she'd been staring into the eyes of another *big man,* a dangerous-looking stranger. But now she knew it hadn't been the danger she'd reacted to, but Blu duFray's silent promise. He had beckoned her to come to him, and she would be forever grateful for that.

Only now, as badly as she wanted to stay, she knew she must leave. Tomorrow night she would be on that bus headed for Nashville. And from there…

It didn't really matter where she ended up. Her heart would always be here with Blu. But as long as Amanda was safe, and she was able to stay one step ahead of Salva, she wouldn't ask for more.

Patch patted the file on his desk. "It's all there. Every dirty little secret Maland owns."

"And Kristen Harris—"

"Is an alias."

Blu turned from the window in Patch's office. He was in a bad mood, possibly the worst mood he'd ever been in in his life. And the Blu Devil in a hell-fire mood with nothing to lose was a deadly combination. "You're sure?"

"It's all there." Patch motioned to the file, then went back to studying Blu's dirty clothes. "You smell like rotten fish. Did I say that already? Ain't no money in that. I smell liquor, too. Dead fish and whiskey. It's a sour mix," he griped.

Blu hadn't bothered to clean up. He'd been working on the *Demon's Eye* when Patch had sent for him. He'd poured himself into the dirtiest job he could find to try to work off some of his anger, but it hadn't helped.

He'd been a fool to walk out on Angel yesterday after he'd said he wouldn't. He'd just been so damn shocked when she told him she was Maland's wife, he'd needed some air. Then he'd needed a drink—more than one. By the time he'd pulled himself together and returned to the *Nightwing,* she was gone.

He'd searched for her, but he hadn't been able to find her. Not yet, he hadn't, but he would. If he had to tear apart every house and store in Algiers, he would find her.

"Are you sure you want to get involved in this again?"

Blu heard Patch talking, but he was still swimming in guilt.

"Are you hearing me? Why would you get involved with something that damn near got you killed last year?"

Blu heard the last sentence. "What do you mean, something that almost got me killed last year?"

"Now I only mention this because the publicity didn't do me any favors, either. People are still wondering how a man like you could turn into one of those do-goodies overnight. Actually, I'm still a little puzzled by that myself. You swinging so far left when you got a god-given talent like you do is crazy in my book. My motto is, Use it if you got it—and you definitely got a talent for scaring the living hell out of people, Blu boy. And when you can make four times as much money doing that, why snag shrimp for a living? And you don't have to stink." Patch produced a can of air freshener from a drawer in his desk and sprayed it into the air.

Blu reached for the file.

"Pretty interesting reading in there." Patch set the air freshener down. "Thought they were full brothers, but I guess they're only half."

Blu set the file back on the desk. "Half? What are you talking about?"

"Taber Denoux's only a half brother to Maland. But I guess that don't matter, their blood runs the same color—black as snake oil." When Blu said nothing, Patch's eyebrows lifted. "Don't tell me you didn't know anything about Maland when you name-dropped him two days ago?"

"I didn't know," Blu admitted.

"Then you didn't know when you busted Taber Denoux last year for stealing those kids that you'd shut down a slice of the biggest pie in the Gulf?"

"No."

Patch's brows crept higher. "Maland's a twentieth-century slave trader, Blu boy. He's international. Taber Denoux had a lucrative slice of the pie, but the big man who turns all the sugar into gold is Salvador Maland."

Blu couldn't believe what he was hearing. "Why doesn't the NOPD know that?"

"Because maybe they don't want to know that."

"I don't believe it."

Patch shrugged. "Maland's a European. He's not a citizen here, and he's smart. He keeps all his dirty business hidden by legitimate import/export companies. Keeps his name off everything."

"Tell me more."

"What you've uncovered, Blu boy, is the motherload. Salvador took over his father's business and has tripled it in ten years' time. Some say he killed his old man to get where he is, others say his mother did it for him. But everybody agrees he's one kinky son of a bitch. He stays clear of the States, or at least he has for the past three years. All the companies are run by independents who know the risks. That's why Denoux's doing time and Maland's still enjoying his island.''

His island. Blu tried to keep his emotions harnessed, but it was getting harder by the minute. He wanted Salvador Maland in an iron box next to his brother and he wanted Angel back on his boat until he could make that happen.

It all made sense now, why Maland had his picture on the wall in his office, why his pictures were in a file labeled *Old Business.* Salvador Maland and Taber Denoux were brothers. Blu could hardly believe it.

''Denoux kept his mouth shut at the trial when he could have cut a better deal for himself?'' Blu heard himself say.

''No sense cutting a deal if you won't live long enough to enjoy it,'' Patch said. ''Salvador Maland is the wrong man to have as your enemy. He's got the longest reach of anyone I know next to God. Brother or not, Taber Denoux would have been dead within twenty-four hours if he had breathed his brother's name. I'm surprised you're not dead yet after what went down last year.''

Blu pointed to the files. ''Somebody sang long and loud for you to get all that on Maland in two days, Patch. Who was it?''

''Now you know I can't give you a name straight out. That's not how things are done. We make an exchange, you go on your way, and you figure out the rest on your own. Say, it was sure nice seeing Lester on his knees the other night crying like a baby. You sure I can't interest you in doing one job a week for me?"

"No. I'm finished with that."

"Then our business is over." Patch watched Blu scoop up the file and head for the door. "You really didn't know, did you?"

Blu stopped at the door. "No, I really didn't know Maland even existed until a few days ago."

Patch pulled his cigarette case from his satin vest pocket. "I figure sometime next week we'll be reading about this on the front page of the *Times-Picayune*. And depending on just how good that god-given talent of yours is, Blu boy, we'll either be calling you the new American hero, or your remains will be in a body bag on the way to the morgue. 'Course, if that happens, Maland will be back selling flesh to the highest bidder from here to Colombia. But only after he carves up that little blond who ran away from him."

Chapter 12

Days ago, Blu had put aside the idea that he'd met Angel somewhere before, and that was true enough—he'd never actually met her. But if the information in the file was correct, then the little tomboy who had been Perch's shadow years ago was more than likely *his Angel.*

Oh, yeah, he knew Perch Aldwin had a granddaughter, had always known. He'd just chosen to forget it because anything involving that crusty old man left a sour taste in his mouth.

Blu slowed the *Nightwing* as he headed around Paradise Point, and there, moored in the bay, sat the pilothouse—the aging old trawler from Perch's heyday when he was king. He'd been a fisherman first, and Blu guessed that's why Perch had become the most respected wholesaler in the area when he'd decided to become a middleman.

He'd lived all his life in Algiers, and the past forty

years on Paradise Point. His wife, Carmela, had died when their only son, Dale, was a teenager. Ten years later, at age twenty-six, Dale, along with his wife, had died in a car wreck. But their children had survived—one boy, and one little girl.

Blu would lay odds that Perch's sudden switch from fisherman to wholesaler years ago had had something to do with the fact that he'd been left alone to raise his two small grandchildren.

It all made sense; Angel's knowledge of boats, her sea legs. She'd grown up with a grandfather who had spent all his life on the water. They had lived on a houseboat, the same houseboat Perch lived on now.

The newspaper article had been labeled, Tragic Drowning On Rough Water. The information claimed that a fast-moving storm had hit suddenly and that the two young people had been too far from shore to save themselves. The paper reported that one body had been recovered—an eighteen-year-old by the name of Benjamin Frank. But the girl, Kristie Aldwin, age sixteen, had never been found.

Sixteen… She'd been sixteen when she'd disappeared, had been working at Smokey Joe's as a waitress the summer she'd supposedly drowned. And for three years she'd lived on an island in the Caribbean with Maland. That would make her nineteen now.

Blu wasn't sure how Salvador Maland had ended up with Angel, but he did know that somehow the sick bastard had managed to either capitalize on a tragic accident, or he had orchestrated the perfect crime.

When Blu saw Perch's small boathouse anchored in a secluded inlet, he cut the engine and steered the *Nightwing* toward the dock. He still needed to be one-hundred-percent sure that *his* Angel and Perch's *Kristie* were one in the same. His gut told him it was true, but he wanted visible proof. And that meant he needed to board Perch's boathouse.

It was early morning, that time of the day when more people were sleeping than awake. But Perch was up. Blu could see him on the aft deck of the boathouse as he tied up the *Nightwing*.

"I need to talk to you, Perch," Blu hollered.

The old man didn't move, he just kept staring out over the water. "You ain't got nothing I want to hear, you black devil."

"I know you and I have had our differences, but this can't wait."

"You don't know how to talk, boy. All you know how to do is throw those fists of yours." This time Perch's head came around slowly. "Your daddy must be moaning in his grave with shame, boy."

Blu saw the scar above the old man's right eye. He'd known facing Perch wouldn't be easy. And he couldn't deny he'd often wondered what his father would have said to a son who had chosen to make money with his fists. Pushing the thought away, not having the time or the energy to contemplate his past mistakes—Blu acknowledged that the sooner he found the proof he was looking for, the sooner he could get back to a more important matter, looking for Angel and Mandy.

"Got a message for Curt. Is he around?"

"No, he ain't. You got something to say to him, you can say it to me. Curt don't like you any more than I do."

Blu kept coming, limping as his long stride ate up the dock. When it ran out, he vaulted onto the deck of the boathouse with one lithe maneuver that easily confirmed his injured leg had never slowed him down. "I guess I'll just have a look around and make sure Curt's not hiding under the bed.''

''No, you won't! You got no right to trespass on me, boy.'' Perch jerked to his feet.

Blu clamped his hand on the man's bony shoulder and shoved him back on the chair. He didn't like playing rough, but if he couldn't get anywhere being nice, then he'd play the role Perch expected him to play. ''Sit, old man, and don't move. I've hit you before, and you know how hard I can hit. But I don't mind showing you again.''

''Bastard!'' Perch continued to cuss, but he stayed down—he was no match for the Blu Devil, and they both knew it.

Inside the boathouse, Blu came face-to-face with a wall covered with dozens of house-blessing masks. He'd forgotten about the masks. Down at Cruger's he'd heard that Perch's collection was second only to Lema's at Spirit World.

A hint of lemon clung in the air, and he turned his head to the left to catch sight of a smoke stream coming from an incense cone sitting on a shelf next to a picture.

A picture…

Blu moved closer, and there in the picture was the proof sitting next to Perch on the old pilothouse. Without a doubt, *his Angel* was *Perch's Kristie.*

Blu felt his throat close off, felt his heart thud loudly in his chest. He left the boathouse seconds later, stepping past Perch without looking at him, then vaulting through the air to the dock. Halfway to the *Nightwing,* still not looking back, he called out to Perch. ''I'll be in touch, old man. Maybe Christmas will come early this year.''

Perch's reply was short and to the point. Two words clearly stated what he thought of Blu duFray.

Kristen woke to the sound of Rose duFray teaching Amanda how to sing "Mary Had a Little Lamb." She quickly dressed in her yellow tank top and fitted jeans, then emerged from the bedroom braiding her long hair into a single plait.

"Good morning, child. Did you sleep well?"

Kristen glanced at Amanda, who was on her knees helping Rose stir a huge bowl of cookie dough. Well, she wasn't really helping, she was stealing nuts whenever the spoon wasn't in motion.

"Amanda, don't do that," Kristen scolded.

"Look, Mommeee, nut." Holding it out to Kristen, she offered her mother the pecan half.

Kristen ate it. "Mmm, it's good, isn't it? But we need to leave the rest for the cookies."

"She's adorable," Rose complimented. "And so smart."

"I want to thank you for letting us stay here last night. And for not calling Blu and telling him we were here."

"I still think that was a mistake, but it was your decision to make."

Kristen dodged the subject. "If you'd like some help in the store for a few hours, I'd be happy to do it. But we'll be leaving later this afternoon."

"Leaving? Where are you going?"

She was beginning to detest the lying. But just once more, Kristen thought. "I have a friend at the women's shelter, Sister Marian. She's expecting us for supper."

"I could use you downstairs after lunch for a few hours. My helper is still sick." Rose turned to the sink, washed and dried her hands, then picked up Amanda and washed her sticky fingers, too. "Look in here, sweetheart." Rose eased Amanda down and opened a cupboard with plastic bowls stacked inside. "You can play with anything you like."

Amanda stretched her little body and looked into the cupboard. When she backed up and looked at Kristen, her eyes were wide and hesitant.

"Go ahead. She said you could."

Of course, Amanda, like any two-and-a-half-year old, was more than eager to make a mess of Rose's cupboard, but messes had never been allowed at the Maland estate. She hesitated a few minutes more, glanced at Kristen again, then finally reached inside and began to empty the cupboard.

Rose poured two glasses of orange juice and brought them to the small table where Kristen sat. "So, what did Blu do to make you leave the *Nightwing?*"

"What makes you think he did something?"

"Because I know my son. I don't like the word 'hot-head,' but he can be ornery and stubborn."

"I haven't really noticed that," Kristen replied. "Not often, anyway."

"Really. That's interesting."

"No. I left the *Nightwing* because I just didn't want to impose on Blu with Amanda." There, that sounded reasonable.

"About Amanda?"

"She's my child," Kristen said quickly.

"I know. She looks just like you. So, Blu didn't ask you to leave the *Nightwing?*"

"No.'

"But you felt you should, and he agreed?"

"Not exactly." Kristen refused to admit the real reason she'd left. "I'm sorry for burdening you like this. I'm going back home in a few days." It wasn't a lie. She was going home, in a roundabout way. Home was where you felt safe and happy, and she intended to find a place where she and Amanda could live without looking over their shoulders.

"If I can do anything… I have plenty of room, child. You can stay here as long as you like." Rose stood, glanced down to where Amanda was enjoying herself building a tower of bowls. "Did Blu tell you about those poor children he rescued last year?"

Kristen was taking a sip of juice. She set the glass down. "No. He never mentioned any children to me."

"That's how he got shot. You knew that he'd been shot?"

"No, I didn't know."

"That's the reason he limps. Didn't he tell you any of it?"

"No."

Rose sighed and headed for the living room. When she returned, she was carrying a scrapbook. "Here. This will give you a clearer picture of who my son really is. You make yourself breakfast and take your time looking through this. That is, if you're interested." She patted the book. "There are things in here that might shock you, but there is more good in here than bad. Anytime the percents are up, a parent should count their blessings. It's a tough world out there, and only the strong make it. I'm proud to say I have two strong children. My husband, Carl, used to say, 'Rose, don't you worry none about those two kids of ours. We grew 'um tough.'"

Kristen was bent over, offering Manard Nelson—a local customer with a round belly and thick glasses—

her advice on spices, when she heard the doorbell ring. She glanced up to greet her next customer and her heart stopped. Blu was coming through the front door. There was no way she could disappear before he saw her, no way to avoid him at all since Rose had slipped upstairs with Amanda for a fifteen-minute break.

She glanced at the clock on the wall. It was three o'clock. The store would close by five, and she'd planned it so she would have just enough time to make it to the bus station by seven.

Manard was saying something. Kristen didn't hear, nor could she move—Blu had spied her and their eyes locked. For a moment she couldn't look away, then she had to. She realized she knew too much about this man, too much and not enough.

"Miss? I said, I'll take the jambalaya seasonin'. The five ounce, please. I'm gonna be usin' it on shrimp and my homemade smoked sausage."

"Good choice, Manard." Blu stepped forward, plucked the spice off the shelf and limped to the cash register. Manard's wrapped fish sat on the counter, and Kristen watched as Blu got busy ringing up the two purchases. She watched his hands, a mix of emotions flooding her thoughts.

"That'll be nine dollars and sixteen cents, Manard."

The older man had waddled to the register. Squinting at the cash register's highlighted numbers, he said, "Don't that seem high?"

"You don't want the spice." Blu reached for the spice and hauled it back, then shoved the fish toward Manard. "Six dollars and forty-nine cents."

"Now wait a minute, Blu."

"Either you want the fish or the spice, Manard. Me,

I'd take the fish. That is, unless you enjoy spicy toast."

"Toast. Hell, I gotta have more than toast for supper. But Pearl said I should pick up seasonin' for her shrimp."

Kristen watched Blu shove the spice forward to join the wrapped fish. "That'll be nine dollars and sixteen cents, Manard."

The older man screwed up his face, looked at the register's highlighted numbers once more, then mumbled something about the high cost of living. Seconds later he dug deep in his pocket and pulled out the correct amount. Blu tossed the money in the till, then came around the counter. He stuck the spice in Manard's shirt pocket, then tossed him the wrapped fish. Manard was still juggling his package as Blu gripped his arm and propelled him out the door and into the street. "Thanks, Manard."

Before the man could reply, Blu shut the door in his face, flipped the Open sign around, then locked the door.

"You can't close," Kristen insisted. "The sign says Open Until Five."

"When you're in business for yourself you can do any damn thing you want. Look at me, I haven't worked for over a week."

His confession reminded Kristen as to why that was, and she raised her chin. "Go back to work, Blu Devil. There's no reason not to anymore."

He studied her a minute. Finally he said, "You didn't have to leave."

"Yes, I did." Kristen wasn't going to get into it. She'd lied to him and he'd walked out because of it. They both had their reasons for doing what they'd done. And that's how she intended to view Blu's "other job," too. He must have had a reason for becoming the *Blu Devil*. She didn't understand it, but one thing she was sure of was that deep in this man's soul he was a good person.

"I want you back on the boat."

Kristen blinked out of her musing. "How did you know I was here? Did your mother call you?"

"No. I've been going door to door. Arnie Lennon down at the liquor store told me he saw you in here yesterday afternoon. Go tell Ma I'm taking you for a boat ride, then out to supper."

"No, I can't. Blu? Blu!"

Kristen raced after him as he headed for the stairs. He took them three at a time and was inside the apartment before she could stop him.

"Ma!"

"Blu, is that you?"

"Da..."

Kristen had reached the door. Blu was already in the kitchen. Rose was holding Amanda in the rocking chair in the living room. With all eyes on Amanda, they watched as she wiggled off Rose's lap, and with a wide grin, trotted eagerly to Blu. More amazing was watching him hunker down and wrap his big hands around her as she began to climb up onto his knee.

"Hey, Mandy, how's my girl?"

Giggling, her little hands squeezed Blu's cheeks, which made his lips pucker, then she kissed him. He made as if he was going to bite her neck after that, and she giggled louder.

For a moment Rose and Kristen watched without saying a word, then finally Kristen found her voice.

"I'm sorry, Mrs. duFray, but Blu put the Closed sign out and locked the door. I tried to tell him—"

"Blu, how am I suppose to pay my bills if I close early without any warning?"

He looked up as if he'd forgotten that anyone else was in the room—his entire attention had been fixed on Amanda. "You never close early, Ma. Once in a while won't hurt. And as far as your bills go, you pay them as regular as you visit the toilet."

"Blu! The baby's ears."

Kristen watched as Blu bent down and scooped a stuffed rabbit up off the floor. "You kept this old thing?"

"I kept all your stuffed animals." She glanced at Kristen. "He loved stuffed animals so much that he slept with them all piled up on his bed. He was still doing that at age eleven."

"Thanks for sharing that, Ma, but I don't think anyone cares."

Kristen watched as his cheeks deepened in color. The Blu Devil was blushing? Who would have thought that was possible?

After a minute passed he said, "I'm taking Kristen for a boat ride, Ma. You mind keeping an eye on Mandy while we're gone?"

"Not at all." Rose stepped forward and for a moment it didn't look as if Amanda was going to willingly let go of Blu's neck.

Kristen knew the feeling. She had felt that very same way the night he had made love to her. And even now, knowing certain things, her feelings for Blu hadn't changed. She still loved him.

"Are you ready?"

Kristen shook her head. "I told you I can't go. It's late and I have to—"

"Leave in time to catch your bus by seven, right?"

That he knew her plans stunned Kristen into silence.

Rose turned and looked at her. "Bus? You're leaving, child?"

"I—I... Yes. I'm going...home."

"She's not leaving, Ma. She's going to miss the bus because I'm taking her on a boat ride and then out to supper. We'll be back late."

Kristen faced Blu, furious that he was taking charge as if he had the right. "I'm not going anywhere with you. And I certainly can leave town anytime I wish."

"Running's a mistake."

"And staying here is getting me nowhere."

Kristen moved past Blu, took Amanda from Rose and headed into the bedroom. She heard footsteps behind her and when she turned to shut the door in Blu's face, it was Rose standing there. "I'm sorry, Mrs. duFray. You must think I'm terrible, taking advantage of your generosity and lying to your face. Blu's right, I was going to slip off in the night without even a thank-you."

"If that's true, I'd say it was the act of someone who is desperate," Rose said. "Are you desperate, child?"

"Yes. Yes, I am."

Rose reached out and touched Kristen's arm. "Then let my son help, child. I can't imagine trusting Amanda's life or yours with anyone else. In your heart, I think you know that's true."

Kristen lowered her voice. "You don't understand, he and I... We—"

"I think I understand more than you think. My advice, child, is to go on the boat ride, and if you still want to leave tomorrow, buy another bus ticket. What could it hurt to stay over one more day? Unless your feelings for my son have changed since you read those newspaper articles in my scrapbook? In which case, I think you might be wise to catch that bus tonight."

Chapter 13

As Blu steered the *Nightwing* toward Paradise Point, he again wondered what his mother had said to get Angel to change her mind and to agree to have supper with him. He hadn't expected her to willingly walk out of the fish market with him, but he was certainly glad it had worked out that way.

He checked his watch, then glanced over to where she sat a few feet away. She hadn't said a word to him, hadn't even looked his way, but he'd been studying her in small doses. He could see now that she had her grandpa's eyes, could even see a little bit of Curt in her—they had the same hair color.

The evening was warm and the friendly music coming from the waterfront was meant to lure boats ashore. Blu backed off the accelerator as they rounded the point and the little fishing community of Crawford's Corner came into sight. Turning the *Nightwing* toward the pier, he said, "We'll eat here," then gestured to the old barbecue shack known for its mouth-watering ribs and the best sweet-potato steak fries on the point.

He watched as Angel assessed the shack with its sagging screen door and aging front porch. He wondered if the place seemed familiar, but she didn't say anything, just stared.

It dawned on him that she just might be viewing his choice of restaurants with disappointment. Angel had spent three years being waited on by maids and cooks, and though she hadn't been brought up that way, he reminded himself that she couldn't remember those simpler times.

He said, "The place doesn't look like much from the outside but Smokey sure can barbecue ribs."

His comment took her attention away from the shack and brought it to him. "This place reminds me of a small eatery on the island. Like this, it never looked like much from the outside, but the islanders always said it had the most wonderful food. Salva..." She looked back at the rib shack, "Salva never let me go there. I tried to tell him that good food wasn't about how shiny the windows were, but who was in the kitchen cooking. Only he never agreed to take me there." She slid off the leather seat and came to her feet. "Do you know if they have crab cakes on the menu?"

The question surprised him, and Blu found himself smiling. He never smiled in public. It was Margo's pet peeve—his sister had call it his inhuman side. But showing emotion in public hadn't fit his old line of work. And even now, though he hadn't worked for Patch for a year, he found it difficult to let himself relax.

Reining in his smile, he said, "I know for a fact that

crab cakes are on Paul Fallow's menu. He hasn't changed it in ten years.''

She didn't appear to recognize her old boss's name, just like she hadn't second-glanced any of the landmarks where she'd grown up. That hadn't been the reason Blu had brought her here—to force her memory—but he had been prepared for it if it should happen. Actually, he had mixed emotions about it. Oh, he wanted her to remember, just not yet—not until he had Maland bagged.

''They're not mushy, are they?''

''What?''

''The cakes? Mushy?''

Blu shook his head. ''No.''

''Then I'm sure I'll like them.''

She was suddenly ahead of him, out of the boat and on her way to the front door. Blu followed with one sure-footed leap to the dock that put him a half stride behind her. His eyes locked on her jeans-clad backside and he took a moment to appreciate the small perfect shape, then his mind was moving on, remembering a few nights ago when she was straddling him and...driving him, his hands all over her satin-smooth curves.

In an instant he was stone-hard, the memory kick-starting his heart rate and sending his blood on another race throughout his body.

The reality was that he wanted her again. Badly. Now. In an hour. After midnight. Tomorrow. The next day, and the next. It didn't matter when or where, or how often, Blu decided, he would never be able to get enough of her. She was flowing through his veins now. He was definitely struggling with the physical end of *loving her,* but it went a whole lot deeper. While one side of his brain wanted to keep Angel in his bed twenty-four hours a day, the other side wanted to keep his promise to her to send Maland to hell and set her free—free as a bird.

And as birds so often do, they fly away. Blu admitted he wasn't ready for that, but he would have to be, because the one thing he was going to do was put Angel's needs first.

He caught up to her on the slat-board steps and they scaled them together. He opened the screen door and as he ushered her inside, he took a quick glance around the plain dining room. Most of the tables were taken, but a few remained. There was loud music with a Cajun flavor coming from the back room, and Blu bent his head to Angel's ear. "You pick," he instructed, then followed her as she chose an out-of-the-way spot near a window that overlooked Paradise Point.

They settled into their chairs. A waitress appeared a minute later, delivering water and menus. When she returned, Angel ordered crab cakes, and Blu chose the barbecue ribs and sweet-potato fries. Alone again, she said, "So why am I here, Blu Devil? For what reason have you decided to take a married woman with a child and no memory out to supper?"

She was back to using his nickname and it irritated Blu more than he would have liked. "We need to talk," he drawled. "To settle this."

"'This'? Which 'this' are we talking about?"

She was too cold suddenly. Blu reached out and stole her hand. "Dammit, stop going for my throat, and listen."

She pulled her hand away and tucked it in her lap beneath the table. "You left, damn you. You said you wouldn't, and then you turned and left. Well, I'm going to leave, too.''

Her face revealed her disappointment, how much his leaving had hurt her. As youth often does, she had vented quickly and openly.

It made Blu feel worse than he already did. ''Yesterday I went out for some air and when I got back you were gone. I know it looked like I was walking, but I never—''

''Liar.''

Blu swore softly. ''I needed air. It was a helluva shock, dammit.''

She stared out the window. ''Imagine lying in a stranger's bed and being told that kind of news. Then learning a few weeks later that you're pregnant.'' She faced him again. ''Yes, I'd say, it was a helluva shock.''

Her point hit Blu square between the eyes, and he felt like a royal ass. He reached out and snared her other hand—the vulnerable one she hadn't buried in her lap. He brought it to his lips and, forgetting that the Blu Devil didn't kiss in public any more than he smiled, he pressed his lips to the back of her hand. ''I'm sorry, baby.''

It was at that exact moment that Curt Aldwin stepped into the dining room. Blu caught sight of Angel's brother out of the corner of his eye while his lips were still pressed against her hand. He released her slowly, watching as Curt's gaze locked on him, then shifted to his sister. On recognition, his face turned the color of a corpse ready for the morgue. He scrambled for the back hall moments later.

Blu knew where the hall led. ''I'll be right back.

Don't go anywhere.'' He eyed Angel a moment, added, ''Say you'll be here when I get back.''

''I'll be here. You said the crab cakes weren't mushy.''

Her comment made him smile, but by the time Blu had made it down the back hall he was stone sober. He found Angel's brother in the bathroom splashing cold water on his face. As Curt looked up from the sink, Blu's image filled the mirror.

''Oh, Jesus!''

''You don't look so good, Curt. You look like you've just seen a ghost.''

''How did you get hold of her? Does she know that I—''

''That you sold her out?'' Blu's eyes turned black.

''*He* said she would have everything she could ever want. That she'd live like a princess.''

''Keep singing.'' Blu put his hands on Curt's scrawny shoulders and squeezed.

''Okay, I accepted money. I admit it. I needed the cash, dammit!''

Blu squeezed harder. ''Keep talking.''

''Ah-hh! I—I told Maland when and where she would be on the water with Ben that day. But I swear, I wasn't involved in killing Ben. I didn't know about that until after. I swear!''

So it hadn't been an accident, after all. The storm had blown in at the right time. Salva had gotten lucky. Blu dug his thumbs into the cords of Curt's neck. ''How much did you sell her for, you bastard?''

Curt groaned, blinked to stay conscious. ''Twenty! Twenty thousand. You're dead,'' he gasped in pain. ''You put Salva's brother in prison. Now you're messing with his property. You're so dead.''

Blu felt an overwhelming urge to break every bone in Curt Aldwin's body. But that didn't fit into his plans, and so he settled for a left to Curt's midsection. Angel's brother crumbled like a dry muffin. Then he half lifted, half dragged Curt into a bathroom stall and slammed him down on the toilet. "You stay there, Curt. Don't go nowhere. Someone's going to come and take you for a ride. You be sitting right there when he shows up, understand? Or do you want me to break both your knees to make sure?"

"Oh, God! Oh, Jesus! I'm going to be sick!"

Blu stepped back as Curt leaned over and puked. Smiling inside, he decided there were days when he did enjoy being the Blu Devil.

"I'll stay," Curt promised, wiping his mouth on his sleeve and holding his stomach as he hung on the edge of the toilet seat. "I'll stay."

"You're smart, Curt. That is, for a dumb little son of a bitch. You better start praying that things turn out *my* way from here on out, or you'll be scraping more up off the floor than your liver. You think about that while you're waiting for my friend."

Blu used the phone in the hall, then returned to the table. Five minutes later he watched as Brodie Hewitt sauntered into the eatery and made his way to the men's bathroom at Smokey Joe's.

As muscular as Blu, but not quite as tall, the foreman for the duFray Devils took one look at Curt, then swallowed the toothpick he was picking apart with his teeth. "You should have flushed yourself, boy, while you had the chance. It might have been a tight fit, but where you're goin', the smell's twice as ripe."

* * *

Life's a dance, Krissy. You keep moving and don't look back. Just keep moving. Dance forward, Krissy. Always dance forward.

Kristen had just finished her crab cakes when the voice—an aging male voice—recited the words inside her head. She sat back and let the plain-spoken words send a shiver up her spine. She knew the voice, knew it for its comfort capabilities. But there was no face or name to go with the liquid-warm comfort that wrapped around her heart.

She glanced around, wondering if this place had opened up a memory vein inside her head, but there was nothing else. Nothing.

"Angel? Did you hear me?"

Kristen shoved her braid off her shoulder and focused on Blu. "I heard. You want me to let you call the shots for the next forty-eight hours. Why?"

"I'm waiting on some information. It's going to take a couple of days to hear back."

"Information?" Kristen couldn't help but look surprised. "From who?"

"I can't say."

She glanced at the bandage on his arm, then the faint red mark still on his neck. Suddenly Kristen understood. Blu had called her naive. And she had been until now. "How do I know you're not lying just to keep me in town?"

"And why would I do that?"

Kristen didn't have an answer.

"I told you before—"

She cut in. "You told me that you're the right man to trust. I know what you said. But you didn't tell me why. What makes you so special, Blu Devil? Why should I trust you over anyone else? Come on, tough guy, what's your secret?''

She waited for him to tell her, but she knew he wasn't going to. For some reason he didn't want her to know about his past. Why?

''Give me two days.''

''That's it? That's all you're going to say?''

''No. I don't think I mentioned Tiny yesterday. He was the guy at Lema's we named the Hulk. Remember?''

''You don't have to explain about Tiny. Sister Marian already told me about her brother and why he was chasing after me that night you...'' Kristen hesitated because all she could think of to say was *That night you kissed me.* And she wasn't going to mention anything physical that they had shared. Finally she said, ''Sister Marian said she sent him after me to watch my backside. Ah, I mean...''

One of his dark eyebrows arched, then he did something totally unexpected—he smiled again. ''Did you tell the good sister it wasn't necessary? That you already have the *Devil* watching your backside?''

Kristen glanced around and caught several women watching them—or rather, watching *him.* Their sudden interest was more than just mild curiosity, and she knew why—Blu's smile was breathtaking. The women were as surprised and fascinated by the sexy smile as she was. She said, ''Close your mouth.''

''What?''

Kristen didn't want him to know she was having a moment of jealous rage, so she tried for sarcasm. ''I don't think this crowd is used to being blinded by the sight of your teeth.''

She had no reason to feel the slightest bit jealous. Feeling possessive of him was just plain stupid. To hide what she was feeling, Kristen directed her gaze out the window.

"What's wrong?"

She could feel the heat from his eyes, knew he expected her to answer. Well, that was too bad—she preferred to continue to stare out the window in silence.

"Angel?" His hand reached out and took hold of her chin and gently turned her back to face him. "You've got that look again."

Kristen knocked his hand away. "That look again? What look is 'that look'?"

"It's the *look* that goes with *that voice.* It's the one that tells me we're not communicating on the same level."

"Oh, I don't know. Your communication skills appear to be fine. Just ask those women at the next table. They can't take their eyes off you."

He was smiling again, and too late, Kristen realized she'd allowed her jealousy to reveal too much.

"You ready to get out of here?"

"And go where?" Her voice still sounded like "that voice."

"Somewhere I can kiss you without anybody watching."

"What?"

Kristen didn't remember getting to her feet. She vaguely recalled Blu paying the bill and leaving a tip for the waitress. Then they were through the door, walking side by side toward the *Nightwing.*

Twenty minutes later Blu dropped anchor in a cozy little bay away from the outside world. The sun had set and what remained was a pale pink sky that promised calm waters and a warm night. Kristen stood at the railing, knowing what was about to happen.

She watched him come toward her. He said, “About that kiss you promised…”

Kristen felt her stomach tighten, felt her entire body turn warm and anxious. “Blu…”

“Shh. We'll talk later.” He brushed her braid off her shoulder and dipped his head. “Right now I need this…” He kissed her slow and careful, his hands wrapping around her. He moved his lips over her jaw, along her neck, dragged her closer into his heat. Kristen could feel him, hard and throbbing against her. She moaned, then gasped when he gyrated his hips to brand her with his hunger. “I need tonight,” he whispered. “I've never needed anyone or anything in my life, Angel. But tonight, I need you. Say yes, baby. Let me love you.”

There was no way she could say no. Her body was already turning into a fire box. “Yes,” she murmured. “Love me, Blu.”

He turned her around and pulled her back into his groin. His head dipped again, his warm lips finding her neck at the same time his fingers found her zipper. He slid it down and shoved her jeans wide. Then his big hand was moving past her panties, and his fingers were sliding into her nest of blond curls.

“Blu…”

His fingers dipped farther. “You're wet.”

“I know.”

“You want me. Say it.”

“I want you, Blu. Please.” Kristen closed her eyes, unable to deny how badly she ached for him. She moaned pathetically as one long finger sank into her. “Take me below,” she pleaded into the sultry night air. “Take us to heaven.”

She was in his arms in a heartbeat. He carried her

downstairs and moved through the dark galley and down the hall. In his bedroom, he laid her on the bed and flipped on the small wall light. He stripped her first, then his own jeans and T-shirt were on the floor. Beautifully naked, he climbed onto the bed. On his knees, straddling her, he towered above her. "You can stop me if you need to," he murmured, then kissed her parted lips, filling her with his tongue.

His mouth moved to her breasts, licking her nipples until they were tight and aching. Kristen moaned softly, arched.

"Remember, you can stop me, if—"

"Never. I don't want you ever to stop."

His tongue explored her navel, his hair moving against her breasts to tease her into another moan. "You smell good," he whispered. "Taste good, too." His fingers parted her, then were replaced by his tongue. Kristen arched off the bed as a primal need sent her passion soaring.

"Blu!"

"I know, heaven, right? Let it take you, baby. I'll be here to catch you on your way back down."

He sent his tongue over her sensitive, hot flesh, branding Kristen with a scalding wave of sweet surrender. She cried out, arched her back. Then she was lost, lost in a delicious thunder and lightning climax that sent her to *heaven.*

And true to his word, Blu was there to catch her as she splintered back to earth.

Chapter 14

It was midnight, and Kristen sat at the kitchen table wrapped in a sheet, watching Blu as he roamed his kitchen like a man who intended to be a bachelor for the rest of his life. He was comfortable in a way that both surprised her and alarmed her. He was definitely a man, who, as he'd said earlier, didn't need anything or anyone to survive.

As he carried scrambled eggs to the table on a plate with one fork jammed into the fluffy pile, Kristen's gaze was drawn to his hip-hugging cutoffs and the scar on his thigh. The wound was close to a year old, from what she remembered reading in the newspaper article—a permanent scar that had left the muscle sunken in, which explained why he limped. The paper claimed he could have lost his leg if the ordeal had dragged on another day.

When he slid the plate onto the table, she redirected

her attention to his handsome dark eyes. Smiling, she asked, ‘‘Are you feeding me?’’

‘‘I cooked. You’re feeding *us*. If we’re going to survive the night, we’re going to need the protein.’’ He placed two glasses of water on the table, then sat beside her. Leaning close, he stole a kiss. ‘‘You okay? Feel all right?’’

What he was asking her was if she was sore or if he’d hurt her. But he hadn’t hurt her, not at all. And if she was sore, it was a good kind of awareness that reminded her of just how much she loved this man. He was always careful, even when the passion stole his breath and made him human. It was the one thing that continued to convince Kristen that Blu duFray was a good man, a decent man.

Look for a man who is good clean through, Krissy. Be picky, darlin’. Make sure he’s good, bone-deep.

The aging male voice was back, but like before, no familiar face or name followed the wise words spoken. Kristen picked up the fork loaded with eggs. ‘‘I’m fine. More than fine. Now, open your mouth.’’

She offered him the eggs and he ate them. While he sipped coffee between mouthfuls, he said, ‘‘We need to talk, you think?’’

‘‘Yes,’’ Kristen agreed. ‘‘We need to talk.’’

‘‘Before or after I make love to you in the Gulf.’’

‘‘In the Gulf? It’s dark out.’’

‘‘I won’t let anything happen to you.’’

‘‘I know.’’ Then she set down the fork and opened the sheet.

It was after midnight when Kristen followed Blu back into the bedroom. ‘‘I thought we were going to talk,’’ she said, swatting Blu’s hand away from her backside.

They had spent an hour making love in the Gulf. Then Blu had talked her into sharing the shower. It had rained heaven in that small shower for another hour.

"We can talk in here."

"But we won't talk, will we?"

He grinned. "Sure we will."

Kristen eyed his powerful naked body as he sprawled on the bed, his long, durable legs spread wide, his arousal already on the move.

She picked up her panties. "We're going to talk."

"As soon as you come here," he agreed. "Forget those." He gestured to the silk in her hand.

"Blu..."

He didn't beg, didn't say anything more. He simply looked at her, the heat in his eyes melting her insides. Kristen dropped the panties and slipped into the bed on her hands and knees. Without reservation, she crawled between his legs, snuggled into him, and laid her head on his hard chest.

Neither spoke as Blu began to stroke her hair. Finally he said, "Tomorrow I want you to stay on the *Nightwing*. I don't want you going anywhere." He tilted her chin to look down at her. "Promise me. You'll give me forty-eight hours."

There was something in his heavy voice that alarmed her, and Kristen sat up. "You know more than you're telling me. This so-called information... You have it already, don't you?"

He tried to pull her back against him, but Kristen refused to be placated. She scrambled off the bed before he could stop her. "Tell me, dammit! I deserve to know what's going on."

"I've got it on good authority that Salva will be showing up here in a day or two."

"He's coming?" She mumbled the words, felt a chill race the length of her spine. "And when were you going to tell me this?"

He swung his legs to the floor. "I wasn't going to if I could help it."

Furious, she snapped, "I had a right to know the minute you found out. This is my life. Mine and Amanda's. I have a right to know everything, damn you! Everything about who you really are, too."

"What's that supposed to mean?"

"Don't play stupid. I know about...about your other job."

He went very still. "Just what do you think you know?"

"'Trust me,' that's what you said. 'I'm the right man to trust.' Well, I know your secret, Blu. I know why you could make that claim. Why didn't you trust me enough to tell me?"

"Dammit!" He was off the bed in an instant. "If you know, then why in hell did you let me—" He gestured to the bed. "We just spent hours there." He turned his back on her and went searching for his jeans. Pulling them on, he spun around. "How did you find out?"

"Your mother."

"What!" His shock was obvious. "She told you that I— What exactly did she say."

"She didn't actually say anything." Kristen gauged his growing anger, worried now that she'd made a grave mistake by bringing it up. "Your mother keeps a scrapbook on each of her children. She offered yours to me to look through. There were newspaper articles and pictures. Last year when you got shot saving those kids... Well, it was all in the scrapbook."

He swore. Crudely.

"Tell me why."

He glared at her. "Why what? You seem to know everything. There's nothing else to say, is there?"

The look in his eyes... What was that? He was angry, but there was something else. "Blu, please. You asked me to trust you. Can't you just trust me a little? I'm not putting you on trial here. I'm just trying to understand who you are." When he said nothing, she stomped her foot. "Dammit, Blu, talk to me!"

"I need some air." He turned to the door.

"No. No, you don't!" Kristen beat him to the door. As if she had strength enough to keep him her prisoner, she braced her hands on either side of the door jamb. "You're not walking this time! You're not! Do you hear?"

"I did what I did. I had my reasons. They weren't the best, but I made a decision and I'll live with it. This is as good a time as any, I guess, to have you find out what I am. This will be over in a few days anyway."

"Over? What does that mean?"

He jammed his hands into his back pockets. "God! Get out of my way. I need some air."

"You'll get your damn air when I get what I need," Kristen insisted.

He gave her his devil's stare.

"That's not going to work on me. I'm not afraid of you. You won't hurt me. It's not in you to hurt me. That other man doesn't exist for me."

He went still. "Don't look at me like that. I'm no damn hero, like those stupid newspapers claim. You think saving those kids makes everything I did all right? Believe me, it doesn't. My hands are more than just a little dirty, baby. You can't just send me through the wash a couple of times and clean me up like a pair of pants. Don't buy into that newspaper crap. I've sent men to the hospital with broken jaws and busted ribs. I've spilled more blood in the street than you will ever see in your lifetime. The best damn enforcer in the city.'' He pointed to the bed. ''You just slept with the city's finest, Angel. How does that make you feel?''

''It makes me feel...'' Kristen raised her chin. ''I feel lucky, and safe. Even though Salva is coming here, I feel safe with you.''

Her answer stunned him, and he turned away. ''You're crazy.''

Crazy in love, Kristen wanted to say. But she didn't. He wouldn't accept that from her right now. He was too busy trying to make her hate him. Why, wasn't clear. ''You saved six kids from a fate worse than death. That makes you—''

''Smart.'' He spun around. ''There was a fat reward! I did it for the money.''

''So you knew about the reward when you decided to hide those kids and stay with them for four days with a bullet in your leg?'' Kristen knew he didn't. The newspaper had written a separate article on one of the kidnapped children. It seemed she was the daughter of a prominent figure out east. He'd offered a sizable reward after the fact.

''Can we get off this damn subject?''

Kristen watched him as he began to prowl the small room like a caged animal. ''The paper claimed you went to work for the loanshark to save your father's fleet. It said the duFray Devils were in a financial crisis and that—''

He stopped and glared at her. "Don't be so naive. I wanted easy money and I found a way to get it."

Kristen studied him for a moment. His body was tense, his jaw set. She shook her head. "No, I don't think it was ever easy for you, Blu. I think it bothered you every day, and it still does. Maybe there was another way to get the fleet solvent, I don't know. What I do know, is that it wasn't based on easy money, or a violent man finding his niche."

He swore again, this time in a string of crude adjectives that scalded the air inside the small room. "You don't know squat!"

"I know that when you make love to me I feel like a fragile piece of glass. There is no selfishness, no violence. I don't feel frightened, or ashamed. I know that inside, you are a good man." Kristen flinched at the depth of pain she saw in his eyes. "I won't hate you, Blu. I'm angry with you for shutting me out, and not telling me the truth about this and Salva, but I can't hate the man I—"

The sound of a boat moving in fast snapped Kristen's mouth shut. She noticed that Blu didn't seem to be alarmed. "Are you expecting someone?"

He didn't answer, he simply found her clothes and tossed them on the bed. "Get dressed, then stay here. Don't come up." Then he turned and left.

On deck, Blu greeted Brodie Hewitt. "You're early."

"Curt got away about an hour ago."

"I thought I said not to let him escape until dawn. That puts everything six hours ahead of schedule."

In the moonlight Brodie Hewitt looked like a badass biker who had bought nine lives and had spent eight.

His premature gray hair, and the age lines around his eyes acknowledged he'd once been either a hard-partying fool, or a man who had seen the dark side of hell more than once. "I know, but the slippery little bastard hit Mort over the head and took off."

Blu rubbed his jaw, calculating the change into his plan. "How is Mort's head?"

"He's got a lump and a nasty headache. He feels like he's let you down. Other than that, he'll live. So now what?"

"It's a given that Curt's going to call Maland and that's what we want. It'll all just happen six hours sooner than we first planned. We can still do it. This might even be better."

Blu wasn't going to explain why that was. He'd set the time frame for selfish reasons so he could be with Angel a little longer. But now that she knew who he really was, it hardly mattered when Curt made his call to Maland. The time he had with her had come and gone. It was too short, but then he would always feel that way. He could spend a lifetime with her and still think it was too short.

"This is a helluva plan, Blu. You sure you want to play it this way?"

Blu looked out over the water. "It'll work."

"It could get you killed."

"Maybe."

"Mort tells me she's a real looker."

Blu smiled a little sadly. "*Oui,* she's some beautiful woman."

He felt Brodie's hand on his shoulder. "Are you sure you want it this way? You don't have to be the one to face Maland. It could be me."

Blu faced his friend. "Thanks, but Maland and me,

face-to-face, that's how it has to be to work. How I want it to be."

"Then we'll do it like you said."

"When this thing goes down, I want Angel in your back pocket far away from Maland. I don't want her anywhere near him."

"It's your party, *mon ami.* Like I said before, we'll do it any way you want it."

"Then I'll see you later."

"Wait a minute. Where are you going?"

"I need some air."

"Did you warn her that I was going to take her back to Rose's place?"

"No."

"Then don't you think—"

Blu vaulted into the boat that drifted alongside the *Nightwing.* "Make sure she gets to Ma's safe and sound, then meet me back on the *Demon's Eye.*"

Salva Maland stood on the deck of the *Princess* and gazed at the yacht's figurehead. Yes, his beautiful princess was naked, her hands tied like he always enjoyed seeing her. He closed his eyes and imagined stroking her jutted-out breasts, mounting her youthful hip.

She was perfection, *his Princess,* and the craftsmen who had spent months creating her flawless likeness had been a master with wood.

The more time that passed, the more Salva realized his mother had been right to warn him about the spell this lovely creature had woven around him. His craving for Kristen had become a fever inside him. She'd become his drug, and he knew—had known for three years—that she was the only woman who could sate his unusual appetite.

His cell phone rang. Salva reached into his pocket and opened the compact phone. ''Is that you, Aldwin?'' he asked as he held the phone to his ear and recognized the man's annoying Southern drawl. ''What the hell do you want? I've just finished tearing apart the Florida coast, and I'm in no mood to—''

''She's here.''

Salva went stone still. ''You have her?''

''No. But I know who does. You're not goin' to believe it, or like it much, though.''

Salva's heart started to pound beneath his expensive black silk shirt. Kristen was in Algiers. How? Why? The only way she could have found her way back there was if her memory had returned. ''Then she knows who she is? She knows about being kidnapped? About our deal?''

''See, that's the crazy part I don't get. If she knew her name, she would have contacted the old man. She hasn't done that. And last night she looked straight at me and didn't recognize me. How she got hooked up with *him,* is a mystery.''

''*Him?* Who are you talking about?''

''The Blu Devil. She was with duFray last night. I caught them together.''

Salva was so stunned he didn't have a reply right away. Finally, he asked, ''Define 'caught them together.'''

''You know, sittin' together at a restaurant. I saw duFray kiss her hand.''

He was hearing the words, but Salva was already revising a new, more heinous way, for the Blu Devil to die. The man had been a thorn in his side for a year. He'd helped send his half brother to prison and had jeopardized his lucrative business. His mistake in not taking duFray out immediately was now costing him more than he had ever imagined possible—the Devil had his princess.

Seething, Salva didn't want to ask his next question, but his fixation had him by the throat. "Do you think he's touched her?"

"You mean, had her?"

Salva gripped the phone tighter.

"Hell, I don't know. I can't say it's happened, but I can't say it ain't, neither. Krissy sure turned into somethin' special."

Salva couldn't take anymore. "How much does the Blu Devil know?"

"Too much. He knows she's my sister, and he knows you killed Ben."

"How the hell does he know that? You talked, didn't you, you bastard?"

"They tortured me."

"They?"

"I was taken to one of duFray's shrimpers and some of his men stripped me and put me in the hold with the creepy crawlies. I barely escaped with my life. But I didn't tell them that I'd talked with you, or that you're comin'. You're comin', ain'tcha?"

For an answer, Salva threw the cell phone into the Gulf. A moment later, he instructed his captain to sail for the Louisiana coast.

Kristen and the Blu Devil together. Salva's rage started to build like a tropical storm. He knew that killing them both would be a reasonable solution to this nightmare he was living. But he also knew he couldn't live without his *Princess.* No, she was going back to the island, and he would punish her every day for the rest of her life for leaving him. But first he would teach her the price of betrayal.

The Blu Devil was a dead man. Only before his blood was drained from his body, Salva intended to strip the skin off his back an inch at a time. And while he filleted Kristen's lover, he would make her watch.

Chapter 15

When Blu arrived at the fish market at nine the next morning, the store was filled with customers, and Bessy Turner was doing her best to see to their needs.

Giving the older woman a nod, he scaled the stairs to the apartment he'd grown up in. His mother came into the kitchen when she heard him enter. He noted her face was pale, but she offered him a weak smile. "Amanda's asleep in the bedroom, and so is Kris."

"Kris?"

"I can't keep calling her Child. She has one of her own."

Blu nodded, then looked down at the black backpack that sat by the door. "I see she's packed. Did Brodie explain what's going on?"

"Only as much as you told him to tell me. Do I hear the rest from you now or later?"

Blu touched his mother's cheek. "Later, Ma."

Rose's chin quivered, but she kept it up. "All right,

then. I've always had to settle when it came to you. I didn't think this time would be any different. Kris packed last night for Amanda. I don't understand why they can't stay together, but I suppose you have your reasons.''

''Margo's place is the perfect safe house for Angel, Ma. And Mandy...'' He cleared his throat. ''For now she needs to be at the shelter. Trust me, Ma. I know what I'm doing.''

''Oh, I've never doubted that, son. I told Kris yesterday that if she was desperate, the man she needed was you. I still believe that.''

''You showed her your scrapbook.'' Blu wasn't angry. He'd made his bed, as they say.

''She deserved to know.''

''Yes, she did,'' Blu agreed.

Rose reached up and kissed his cheek, then she stepped back and gave her son a long head-to-toe. ''You certainly grew taller than either Carl or I ever thought you would.'' She patted his chest, her hand lingering. ''I don't know why all this is necessary, but I trust you'll get around to tell me as soon as you get a spare minute. Until then, I'll just go along with whatever it is you want done.''

''Thanks, Ma. I can always count on you. And I appreciate your faith.''

Blu tried to keep the worry from his eyes. His mother was perceptive and he didn't want to upset her. He wished Margo was there in case things turned sour. His mother would need her if... He gripped her arms and leveled his gaze on her. ''I need you strong, Ma. Don't sell me short. I'm the Blu Devil, remember?''

The sound of the bedroom door opening caught Blu's attention, and he watched as Angel walked into the kitchen carrying Mandy. Her hair was tousled, and she had that heavy-lidded look that told him she'd just woke up.

"Amanda heard your voice." She shifted her daughter to her hip.

Blu studied the two blond beauties who had entered his life so unexpectedly. If only things had turned out different, he thought. But fate had a way of shifting the tide, and knowing there wasn't much time left, he put to memory everything about his two girls—their pretty brown eyes and small sweet mouths. Their fragile innocence.

"Da, come home."

Suddenly Mandy wiggled out of her mother's arms. Blu watched her come to him. He felt his throat close up as he bent and scooped her up. She was warm and soft and she smelled like lemon verbena, just like her mama. He felt the lump in his throat grow bigger, and he turned away from Angel and his mother to give himself a minute to pull it together.

A moment later he turned back to return Mandy to her mother, but she had other plans and clung to him. She tried to bite his chin, then giggled.

"Mandy," Angel scolded, "you don't want to hurt Blu."

It didn't take much to crush Mandy's feelings. Her mother's words had her pulling her hands back close to her chest and hanging her head.

"She can't hurt me," Blu insisted. When Mandy didn't lift her head, he pulled her close and started nibbling on her ear until he had her giggling hysterically.

"Blu, how is she going to learn proper behavior if you let her do anything she wants?"

He directed his attention to Angel. "There's time enough for her to learn proper behavior. Right now all she needs is to feel safe and happy."

The words reminded Blu that if Mandy was ever going to have a chance for a normal childhood, he had places to go and people to see. He hugged her close, then handed her back.

Angel took her, but just as quickly handed her to his mother. "I need to talk to Blu, Rose, could you keep Amanda occupied for a little bit?"

"Of course."

She turned back to the bedroom and Blu had no choice but to follow. As he stepped inside, she closed the door behind him. Glancing at his watch he said, "Brodie will be by in about two hours to take you to my sister's house. Mort will—"

"Why did you leave last night?"

Blu kept his distance. He wasn't going to touch her, he'd already decided that. He needed his head clear and his thoughts only on Salvador Maland. "I needed air. You know me. I walk easy."

His words hurt her, but it was for the best. She couldn't keep walking around thinking he was something that he wasn't. "Mort will be with Brodie. He's taking Mandy to the shelter. You won't be leaving together, and you'll wear disguises."

"I don't see why we have to split up."

Blu had no intention of explaining. No matter how

much he wished there was a better way to snare Maland, a safer way, this was a solid plan. "I want you to stay at Margo's until I come for you."

"And when will that be?"

"Sometime tomorrow."

"Just like that. I'm suppose to do whatever it is you tell me? I left Belize because I was told what to do every minute of the day. What makes you think I'm going to do what you tell me just because it's you telling me instead of Salva?"

"That's not why you left Belize, and we both know it," Blu countered. "The reason you'll do what I tell you is because you know who I really am, and what I'm capable of. And if you would be honest right now with me and yourself, deep inside you're praying I'm even worse than the rumors claim." When she attempted to speak, he held up his hand. "No. Don't tell me I'm good. The guy you need watching your backside right now, baby, had better be one mean son of a bitch. Because that's the only way you're going to get out of this in one piece. Mandy, too."

"This isn't fair. You're not being fair!" She was crying now, coming undone.

Blu watched her wrap her arms around herself. He had to touch her. Had to ease her fear. He stepped forward, pulled her into his arms. "He won't touch you. I promised you that days ago, and it's still my promise. He won't even see you." She kept crying. He shook her a little. "He's just a man made up of blood and guts like me. He's beatable. The Blu Devil can beat him."

She broke away from him and backed up, shaking her head.

"You can help," Blu heard himself say. "Give me some facts about him. It doesn't have to be much. The yacht. What will he be sailing?"

She was against the wall, clinging to it as if she needed it for support. "He'll be sailing the *Princess.* You won't be able to miss her. She's a beautiful boat, and..."

Her voice broke. Once again Blu was there, pulling her away from the wall and into his arms. "And what?"

"Salva had a man sculpt a figurehead for his yacht. It's me. I'm naked, my hands are tied behind my back. He made me...made me pose for it. The figurehead rides the *Princess.*"

Blu tried to keep his rage below the surface. She must have sensed his struggle. She backed away. "I'm sorry. When I came here all I wanted was to find some way to go back to being whoever I was before...before I woke up and found myself in a nightmare." She paused. "I wanted to go backward, but I know now that's impossible. All I want right now is for you and me to— I couldn't bear it if you got hurt because of me. Please, go to the police. Let's tell them my story, and—"

Blu shook his head. "It's too late for any of that."

"It can't be too late. I love you. I know I shouldn't be saying that now. That you don't want to hear it. And I know I have no right the way things are, but—"

"Don't finish." As much as he wanted to hear her confession of love, Blu couldn't let her go on. He pulled her against him and covered her trembling lips with his own. He knew he needed to distance himself from her, but the need to taste her one last time was stronger.

He kissed her tenderly, then possessively. She leaned into him, gave herself over to him completely—her need as clear as his own.

Blu wanted to possess her, to make everything all right for her and Mandy. And he wanted her to keep on loving him forever. He'd never wanted anything so badly as he wanted a chance for a life with this beautiful young woman. But that wasn't going to happen. As much as he wanted to hold on to her, he wanted her to be free more. He wanted her standing on her own two feet, starting over, and being whoever it was she needed to be.

Blu brushed her long hair off her shoulder and murmured huskily, "I have to go." Then he kissed her one last time.

The moment the door closed, Kristen's knees buckled and she sank to the narrow bed. A vision of Salva flashed in her mind and she began to shake. And that's when she knew that what Blu had said was true—she wanted the Blu Devil to save her and Amanda. She wanted him to rip Salva apart and save them from a fate worse than death.

"Kris?"

The door opened and Kristen dabbed at her eyes and tried to dry her cheeks. "Yes."

Rose came forward, Amanda toddling beside her. "Brodie called. He said he and Mort are on their way."

Amanda wiggled and squirmed until she'd climbed into her mother's lap. Kristen's arms went around her daughter. "You've been very kind, Rose. Thank you for letting us stay in your home."

"Will you be all right while I go down and check on Bessy?"

"Yes."

"All right, then. You wash your face, and freshen yourself up. I'll take Amanda with me. Come on, sweetheart, come with Grandma Rose."

When Kristen emerged from the bedroom an hour later, she found Brodie and Mort sitting at the table with her daughter. They were sharing cookies and milk; Amanda was the server, dunking the peanut butter cookie in the milk, then feeding the snack first to Brodie, then to Mort—they were all sharing the same cookie. Her daughter was laughing as Brodie was trying to eat her fingers along with the cookie.

Kristen stood in the doorway and watched. The men were so taken with her little girl that she again felt like crying. Amanda's life had had so little laughter in it, and she'd been forced to accept so many rigid rules. Here, it was all about feeling safe and being happy, just like Blu had said.

Brodie saw her first, and stood quickly. "You want to join us?"

Kristen nodded, then took the chair between her daughter and Mort. Amanda immediately dunked a cookie in the glass of milk and stuck it in front of her mother to take a bite. Kristen did, and so the game continued.

"Rose is still downstairs," Mort told her around his next bite. "She told us to come up with Mandy."

Kristen glanced at Mort's handsome face, then Brodie's. Last night she hadn't gotten a good look at him. He'd sailed her back to River Bay and escorted her here, but frankly, she'd been too upset with Blu for leaving her to notice anything or anyone. Only now there was time to assess Blu's friends. She'd read in one of the newspaper articles that Mort had been one of the kidnapped kids that Blu had rescued. He hadn't had a home to go back to so the Blu Devil had given him his. She'd also read that Brodie Hewitt had risked his life to protect Margo and Blu during that terrible time. The paper claimed he was lucky to be alive.

Taking in the older man, she noted that Brodie wasn't as tall as Blu, but he was just as tough appearance-wise. Older than Blu, his hair was already starting to turn gray. His green eyes were striking and intelligent, and Kristen liked his rogue's smile. But she wasn't so sure about the unusual tattoo on his arm that depicted a stylized raven.

"We're leaving first," he suddenly told Kristen, glancing her way and seeing that she'd been staring. "Mort will take Mandy to the shelter once we're gone."

Kristen didn't say anything.

Brodie reached for a bag that sat on the floor and put it on the table. "Once you change, we can leave anytime."

Kristen took the bag and peered inside. Along with a red skirt and white blouse was a short black wig and a brimmed straw hat. When she looked back at Brodie, he shrugged. ''You're suppose to look like a customer leaving the store with tonight's supper. Blu's idea. Me, I'll leave first and pick you up a couple blocks up the street.''

Again Kristen said nothing, but then she noticed a similar bag sitting on the floor next to Mort. ''And does Amanda turn into a boy.''

Mort grinned. ''Sure, why not? Blu's—''

''Idea.''

Kristen felt a sudden surge of hope. Maybe all this *was* going to work. Maybe trusting the Blu Devil had been the answer from the very beginning, and that's why she'd been drawn to his picture back on the island.

The *Princess* sailed around Algiers Point at five that afternoon. As Angel had said, Maland's yacht would be hard to miss. From where he stood on the deck of the *Demon's Eye,* Blu sent the binoculars over the bald-headed crew. He kept scanning, in hopes of catching a glimpse of Maland, but after a second, then a third round of detailed scoping, he concluded that the bastard was below deck.

''Wow!'' Mort made a low whistle from somewhere behind Blu. ''That's some fancy boat.''

''*Oui,* some fancy boat,'' Blu agreed, moving his binoculars to the bow where a beautiful naked siren figurehead bucked the wind. It was true, the likeness was incredible. Maland's craftsmen had captured Angel's innocence as well as taken the time to detail three feet of wild, flowing hair.

He'd always known that Angel's abuse had been both physical and mental—that she'd endured a crazy kind of madness few women would have been able to survive. Seeing her image riding Maland's yacht told Blu just how crazy that madness had been.

His stomach knotted in reaction and yet he kept his anger contained. At the appropriate time he would vent his outrage and let it go, but that would be later. It would be a private unleashing, and it would mark the end of Salvador Maland. But for now, while he waited for the next step in his plan to unfold, he would remind himself that Angel had survived Maland's treachery for three long years.

Survived was the important word. Her strength had been quiet, but nonetheless powerful enough to see her and Mandy through the hardest of times. Once Maland was out of her life, she would be all right.

Blu checked his watch. If his plan stayed on schedule, they should be seeing Curt Aldwin within the hour. He pulled his cell phone from his back pocket and called Brodie at Margo's house. As soon as he heard his friend's voice, he said, "How's Angel doing?"

"She's been pretty quiet. That's good, right?"

"Maybe. Keep your eyes on her."

"That won't be hard to do."

"You're not her type," Blu heard himself say.

"Yours, either."

That was true enough, Blu thought. She deserved someone a whole lot better than he could ever be. "She needs a gentle hand," he heard himself say.

"I can be gentle."

"Dammit, Brodie, just keep your hands to home, your fantasy caged, and your eyes open. Got it?"

Brodie chuckled. "I got it. Everything okay on your end?"

"He's here."

"Then he swallowed the bait?"

"It looks that way. Call me if you need something." Before Brodie could irritate him further, Blu disconnected, then punched in another number. "You see what I see?"

"With both eyes. Now we wait."

"That's right," Blu agreed. "Now we wait."

Kristen gauged the distance to the tree from the upstairs window, took a deep breath, let it out slowly, and pitched herself out the two-story window of Ryland and Margo Archard's lovely home in the Garden District. As the sturdy limb came within reach, she wrapped her arms tightly around it and hung on, then swung herself up to straddle the limb.

It was dark out, just barely. The cloudy sky made it seem later than it really was. Kristen took a minute to catch her breath. Her request had been nothing out of the ordinary. It wasn't as if she'd asked to say goodnight to Amanda in person. She had simply asked Brodie if she could phone the shelter and speak to her daughter before she went to bed. But the surprised look on his face when she'd made the simple request had immediately made Kristen suspicious. Then her suspicion had turned to worry when he'd made a lame excuse about Blu telling him they shouldn't use the phone. At that moment Kristen knew she had to see for herself that Amanda was safe at the shelter.

Sitting fifteen feet in the air, Kristen calculated the

best way to the ground then picked her way carefully from limb to limb. Five minutes later she was sucked close to the house, considering her next move. She could walk out the front gate, but Ryland Archard was a cop. What if he had an alarm on his iron gate? So far Brodie didn't know she was gone, and she meant to keep it that way for as long as she could.

The hole in the hedge took a long ten minutes to find, but it was a perfect fit. Looking back, Kristen could see Brodie standing in the yellow kitchen, see that he was talking on the phone. So much for not using the phone, she thought.

His obvious lie brought a wave of fear racing through her. Fear that, as a mother, she had abandoned her child in a dangerous situation and now she would pay dearly for that error. The fear made her anxious, and Kristen began to run. Keeping an eye out for trouble, scanning the streets block by block for a cab, she headed into the heart of New Orleans.

Near Canal Street, she hailed a cab. Grateful when it pulled to the side of the street, she climbed in and shut the door.

The cab driver turned.

Kristen sucked in her breath and started at the man's shiny bald head. She grabbed for the door, had it open when the cabbie said in thick New Orleans fashion, "How y'all doin' this evenin', miss? Where to?"

Kristen hesitated, remembered a similar situation that had caused her to needlessly panic. She relaxed back in the seat, then reached up and fingered the black bangs on the wig that covered her head.

"You feelin' all right, miss?"

Kristen nodded. "Jus' fine," she drawled. "Take me to the women's shelter on Carmel Avenue, please. Carmel in Algiers."

"That's the only Carmel there is, miss. Y'all will be there in fifteen minutes."

True to his word, fifteen minutes later, Kristen paid the cab driver with the little bit of money she'd found on Margo's dresser. As the cab drove off, she hurried up the stairs to the shelter. She was inside, heading for her old room when she glimpsed the back of a man just turning down the corridor ahead of her—a big man. Her heart in her throat, Kristen hurried to the end of the hall. When she got there, no one was in sight. Thinking she was again overreacting, she reached for the doorknob to her old room. She was ready to burst inside, when common sense returned. What if Amanda was sharing Sister Marian's room? What if this was now someone else's room?

Kristen took a deep breath, then rapped sharply on the door. She heard footsteps coming toward the door and she tried to relax. The door opened, and there, to her surprise, stood Blu, wearing a scowl. A moment later he said, "I overlooked one thing. You're a good mother. Of course you would want to check on Mandy before she went to bed. My mistake."

Kristen heard the words, dismissed them as she scanned the empty room. Convinced her daughter was in another room, she demanded, "Where is she?"

His face was void of emotion. Kristen wrapped her arms around herself and took a step back. "I said, where is—"

"Sit down, Angel."

The way he said the words, dread and fear grabbed Kristen by the throat and squeezed. She shook her head, tried to speak. She backed up, tried again to say something.

She heard Blu swear, then he was moving toward her. "Breathe, dammit, you're going to pass out if you don't."

He gripped her arms, shook her. Air filled Kristen's lungs as she fought to regain her freedom. He let go, then stepped away from her.

"You promised me!" Kristen couldn't hold back the tears. "Where's my daughter? Damn you, Blu! Where's Amanda?"

This hadn't been part of his plan, and Blu hated to think of what that meant. Now he would be forced to tell her the truth. He said, "You were suppose to stay at Margo's place. You were—"

"Where's my daughter?"

Blu braced himself for the hate that was about to fill her eyes. "Salva has her."

"Oh, God! Oh, God!"

As her knees buckled, Blu caught her and eased her down onto the edge of the bed. She bent over holding her stomach, and started to moan. Blu watched, helpless to do anything for her.

"I knew it. I knew no one would be able to stop him from taking us back. Oh, God. Amanda... He's got Amanda."

Her pain was sharp, her hate as she gazed up at him was sharper, slicing him into pieces. "I hate you! Hate you!"

"You have that right." Blu kept his voice steady. "But you can hate me from Margo's house. Right now I've got to get back to the *Demon's Eye,*" he said. "I haven't answered Maland's demand yet, and—"

"What demand? How dare you do anything without discussing it with me? Haven't you done enough to me? To us?"

Blu stayed where he was, let her vent.

Suddenly she was on her feet. "Amanda is my child! My life! My future! Oh, God, he has her."

She broke down again, and Blu had all he could do to not reach out to her, to hold her. But she would push him away if he did. He knew that there would never be another chance to hold her, to kiss her, or to tell her that he loved her. He'd always wanted to tell her that.

"I want to see the demand." She stuck out her hand, her pretty brown eyes clouded with tears.

Blu pulled the slip of paper from his pocket and handed it to her. She unfolded it, read it with shaky hands. He waited, wasn't surprised when the frown came. She looked up, still scowling. "He wants to trade Amanda for me? I don't understand. It must be some kind of a trick."

Blu shook his head. "It's no trick. He doesn't want Mandy. Why would he want someone else's child?"

"What?"

Blu hadn't planned to tell her anything until she was free of Maland. Now he knew he had no choice. "Your name is Kristie Aldwin. You're nineteen. You'll be twenty next month. July ninth. You grew up on your grandfather's fishing boat near Crawford's Corner. When you were sixteen you were seeing a guy named

Benjamin Frank. I believe he's Mandy's father. You were kidnapped off his boat in the middle of a storm. Ben Frank drowned. They found his body. They never found yours."

He decided to forget about Curt and the role he'd played in Angel's kidnapping for the time being. She was already looking at him as though he'd lost his mind.

"Salvador Maland is an international slave trader, among other things. But he didn't kidnap you to sell you like the others. With you..." Blu shrugged. "He liked what he saw and decided to make you his. Ironically, he's Taber Denoux's brother—the man I helped put away last year. That's why he had my picture."

"And Amanda is Ben's baby? You're sure?"

"I don't have solid proof. But yes, I believe that's true." Blu hesitated, then came clean. "My old boss, Patch, has a lot of contacts in low places. He was able to get the information for me."

"And he just gave it to you because you asked?"

Blu didn't answer.

"Of course not. I'm being naive again, aren't I? You no doubt went out and pounded some poor man's face..." She sucked in her breath and squeezed her eyes shut. "Oh, God, you did, didn't you? It was the night you came back to the *Nightwing* bleeding and in a sour mood."

Blu didn't deny it, there was no reason.

"Why didn't you tell me this sooner?"

"I planned to give you the files when the time was right."

"And when was that going to be?" She held up her

hand. ''Never mind. I've heard enough. I want you out of here. Go!''

Blu didn't move.

''I said, go!''

''So you can do what?''

''Is my grandfather still alive?''

''Yes.''

''Then I'll make the trade. Amanda will...will be raised by my grandfather and I'll return to the island. At least my daughter will be free.''

Blu studied her tear-streaked face. ''You think I'd let you do that?''

She glared at him. ''This is my choice, not yours. You don't even get a vote. I trusted you once, I won't make that mistake again. I'm going through with Salva's demand. And not you or anyone else can stop me.''

She brushed the tears from her cheeks and set her shoulders—proving to Blu that she was stronger than anyone would ever imagine. ''Salva says I'm to be on the wharf at seven tomorrow morning.''

''Angel, I think—''

''No. You don't get to think anymore, Blu Devil. The demand requires that you accompany me to the wharf. I guess we both know why that is, but it makes no difference. Amanda is the important one in this. When the trade is made, I expect you to honor my wishes and get her to my grandfather. Now go away. I want to be alone.''

Chapter 16

The sunlight made Angel's hair look like pure silk as she reached the wharf. Blu kept pace with her, his eyes glued on Salvador Maland at the end of the wharf. He counted six men with him—the man on Maland's right held Mandy.

She looked scared, but unharmed. Blu found himself silently saying a prayer that she would remain that way. "Not so fast," he growled at Angel. "You're walking too damn fast."

His gaze went back to Salva where he stood in his flowing black pyjamas like some exalted king. Blu tried to relax, but he was having a hard time breathing.

It was time for Angel to hang back and wait. He said, "This is as far as you go for now. If Maland's serious about the trade, he's going to have to send Mandy before he gets you."

Blu's voice was flat, his throat dry. He stopped alongside Angel and scanned the wharf, dissecting the situation. Maland had chosen a congested wharf to make the exchange. The boats going in and out of port would benefit his escape once he had what he wanted. The trick would be to force him into making a mistake.

"Don't move from here until you hear me call to you," Blu insisted, then he started walking again. Thirty feet from Maland, he stopped once more. "I hear Taber's got a new profession in Angola," he called to Salva. "All that long hair and those good looks are serving him well."

He watched Salva's lip curl, watched the man's fist clench. "You got something of mine, Blu Devil. Did you taste it?"

The question wasn't going to get an answer. Blu said, "You killed Ben Frank."

"Can you prove it?" Salva laughed. "That storm came up quick. Quicker than any of us expected. Ben could swim, all right. I could have helped him more, I suppose. But I had my hands full holding on to what I'd paid for."

Blu wouldn't let his anger allow him to lose control. "I'm offering you a new deal. Me for them. You let them both go, and you get me instead."

The proposition seemed to surprise Salva at first, then it angered him. "You messed with her, didn't you? You got her sugar running through your veins." He was quiet a moment, then he admitted, "Ain't it a rush, having her beneath you? She's heaven and hell, Blu Devil. The best there is, and I should know, right? In my profession I'm a connoisseur."

Blu kept his emotions masked. "Do we have a deal?"

"No deal. You can have the brat as soon as I get what's mine."

Blu knew then that he'd been right. Ben Frank was Mandy's father. "I want the kid on the ground, moving this way," Blu insisted, "or the deal's off."

Blu saw Salva shift his gaze to where Angel stood. He licked his lips, his thoughts obviously putting together a warped fantasy or some gruesome punishment for her. Suddenly he signaled the man holding Mandy to step forward. "Let's compromise. My man will walk beside her. Keep her in line."

Blu considered what Maland said. "All right."

Salva nodded, then said, "You're a dead man, duFray. Know that this isn't over after today. We still have a score to settle. Just you and me."

Blu was in full agreement. "You're right, Maland. Today is just the beginning of you and me."

"I'll be waiting on the island. Princess will be waiting, too," he taunted. "But you might not recognize her when you get there."

"Angel," Blu called. "Start walking."

The man who held Mandy set her tiny feet on the wharf. When her bright eyes locked on Angel, then on Blu, she cried, *"Da,"* and started to run toward him.

Her unexpected actions drew Salva's attention, and as Blu took in his enemy's expression, he knew Salva had just realized his error. "She's an imposter," he roared, pointing at Angel.

A half second later Blu hollered, "Mort, get Mandy."

The moment the words were out, Mort—wearing a long blond wig—raced to Mandy and scooped her up beneath his arm. As he raced for cover, Salva shouted, "Kill them. Kill them all.".

As Salva's men produced an arsenal of weapons, Blu quickly took out the man who had been holding

Mandy. A right to his jaw, and the man lay unconscious on the wharf. Then he was calling out to Salva, challenging him in hopes of distracting his men away from Mort and Mandy. His taunts worked and he suddenly found himself dodging bullets as he raced along the wharf in the opposite direction Mort had gone.

Blu heard police sirens moving in fast and knew that Jackson Ward was on top of the situation. His backup squads would be saturating the wharf within minutes, and Maland's yacht had probably already been boarded by the coast guard.

Maland's fury zeroed in on the one man he wanted dead above all else. Half his men had deserted him, but he wasn't retreating himself—his focus was solely on bringing his enemy down.

Blu was in midair, on his way into the water, when he felt the bullets hit him. It didn't matter, he thought, already resigned to whatever Fate had planned for him. The impact shook him, took him farther into the air, then dropped him.

The pain was real. Real enough that it should have grabbed his attention, but as Blu hit the water all he was thinking about was that Mandy was safe and that he'd kept his promise to Angel. She was free as a bird now. And he'd accomplished that without putting her anywhere near Salvador Maland.

Kristie Aldwin had watched everything from a distance onboard the *Nightwing.* She was supposed to be safe at Margo's house with Brodie, but she'd insisted that he take her to the wharf. As she watched the police arrest Salva's men, she recalled the moment she'd seen Mort in his *Angel* disguise appear on the dock with Blu.

From a distance Mort had easily passed for her in the blond wig. It was amazing, but with makeup and the right clothes he had become her.

Never in her wildest dreams had Kristie imagined Blu's plan would work, but he'd given her no choice last night when she'd attempted to strong-arm him into going along with her decision to trade herself for Amanda. Blu had simply swore, then picked her up and handed her to Brodie Hewitt who had been waiting just outside the door, saying, "Take her back to Margo's and this time, dammit, tie her up if you have to."

That was the only time Blu had touched her. Back at his sister's house, he had explained to her that, yes, he'd set it up to have Amanda kidnapped from the shelter. That Mort, dressed in a blond wig earlier in the day, had escorted her to the shelter for that sole purpose. At that point, Blu told her about her brother, Curt, and how he had sold her to Salva three years ago. Then he'd told her that last night Curt had been the one who had taken Amanda from the shelter and delivered her to Salva. Blu said Curt had actually expected to find her there instead of Amanda because he'd been tricked by Mort's disguise, but when she wasn't there, he had settled for her daughter—as Blu knew he would.

Kristie snapped out of her musing as Brodie hauled back on the throttle and brought the *Nightwing* in close to Mort and Amanda. Through her tears, Kristie knew just what to do to rescue her daughter from the river, and she went to work tossing out the life preserver. Once Mort was in the boat and Amanda in Kristie's arms, Brodie had the engine at full throttle once more, in search of Blu.

Blu... As Amanda clung to her mother, her little teeth chattering, Kristie began to scan the water. Blu's valiant effort to draw the gunfire away from her daughter flashed before her eyes, and she again found herself crying. Dread swept over her, along with an enormous amount of guilt for the things she'd said to him last night. She wanted to take them all back, to ask him to forgive her. Was it too late?

They neared the wharf. Kristie could see Salva wrestling with two policemen as they cuffed his hands behind his back. As if some powerful force struck him, he stopped his struggle and turned his head toward the water. His furious gaze found her quickly, and for an instant a strange kind of anguish swept his eyes. Anguish over what he'd lost—was that what she was seeing? Kristie believed it was. And it was then she decided, that in a crazy, bizarre way she would never understand, Salvador Maland had loved her.

A violent chill swept over her with the realization, and she hugged Amanda closer. The radio squawked. Kristie turned, watched Brodie pick up the receiver and speak into it. She watched as his face grimaced, watched as he glanced her way. She knew the report was coming from Jackson Ward, that the information was about Blu.

Then the *Nightwing* was moving off, leaving the wharf and heading for River Bay.

Two days later, dressed in a simple white sundress, carrying her daughter, Kristie Aldwin climbed out of the rented cab and headed for the boathouse at Paradise Point, and the old man who stood anxiously awaiting her arrival on the dock. She didn't recognize him as she focused on his bent-over posture, and that hurt, but it didn't stop her from moving forward, or from wanting to meet her grandpa.

Amanda was chattering, clutching Blu's old stuffed rabbit that Rose had given her. Kristie glanced at it now, wondering where he was at that moment. She hadn't seen Blu since all hell had broken loose on the wharf and Salva had been hauled off to jail by Jackson Ward. She had planned to see him, but then Brodie had told her that Blu, after seeing to his two gunshot wounds, had boarded the *Nightwing* and had taken off. Brodie had claimed that Blu had needed…some air.

She wasn't angry that he'd left, more worried than anything. Brodie had explained that Blu's injuries weren't life-threatening, but that he had been expected to stay in the hospital.

Of course he had rejected that.

After two days the newspapers were still claiming that the Blu Devil was a hero, and Salvador Maland a modern-day pirate who would never see the light of day ever again.

She'd been asked to give a statement at the police station about the past three years, and with Jackson Ward and Brodie Hewitt by her side, she'd managed to tell her story. Along with her confession, she'd learned that Amanda *was* Ben Frank's daughter, and though she couldn't remember him, she was confident that someday she would. She had also learned that she had never been married to Salva. That he'd lied about her being his wife, just as he'd lied about so many things.

If Kristie had any doubts that Perch Aldwin was her grandpa, the look on his face as he locked eyes with her convinced her otherwise. She saw his tears, saw him shaking as she closed the distance between them.

"I didn't believe him," Perch muttered as Kristie stopped on the dock next to the boat. "The Blu Devil,

I mean. He came by and told me the story. I said he was crazy.'' He glanced at Amanda. ''She looks just like you did when you were a baby.''

Kristie wasn't sure what to say, so she chose to say nothing and instead wrapped her arms around her grandpa's aging shoulders and, with Amanda between them, hugged him.

She felt the air in his lungs rush out, knew he was crying again. She said, ''It's okay, Grandpa. We've got lots of time to catch up. I'm not going anywhere.''

Four days had passed since Blu had surfaced in the river with a bullet wound in his leg an inch below last year's wound, and a shoulder contusion where another bullet had grazed him. Four days since he'd spoken to anyone after he'd made a stop at the hospital to see to his injuries, then paid a visit to Perch, and then one to the jail.

True to his word, Jackson had looked the other way when Blu had literally beaten the hell out of Salvador Maland. He had given the man a small chance to defend himself, but in the end, he had limped out of the precinct with his bloody knuckles jammed in his pockets, knowing he'd finished the job he had set out to do—Maland was going to prison with Blu's blessing, and Angel and Mandy were now free.

He docked the cruiser in the old slip that still had his father's name on it, not ready to see anyone just yet. He figured Margo and Ry were back by now and anxious to talk to him—especially since the newspapers had gone wild with the story. He'd managed to pick up a copy of the *Times* each day he'd been gone to keep abreast of the situation, and hadn't been surprised the headlines read, The Crescent City Devil is the Hero of the Day Once More.

Blu shook his head. He certainly didn't feel like a hero. He'd placed an innocent two-and-a-half-year old in danger, and had lied through his teeth to the woman he loved. He felt like scum, and he deserved to feel that way. He'd been way out of line, insisting to Jackson and Brodie that he wanted it all done his way or no way.

His thoughts returned to Angel. He was still having trouble calling her Kristie, and he supposed he always would. He'd talked it over with Jackson when he'd decided to leave for a few days, and his friend had promised to stick by her while the whole mess got sorted out.

Blu headed below deck, limping as he went. His shoulder was doing fine, but his leg was sore as hell. He'd have more of a limp than before, the doctor had told him, but the old injury had never slowed him down, so there was no reason to think this one would, either.

In the galley, he stopped and pulled a bottle of whiskey from the cupboard, then headed into his bedroom. Dropping the bottle onto the bed, he stripped off his clothes and sprawled on the mattress. Tomorrow he would join his crew and get lost in work, but tonight he was going to get drunk.

An hour later Blu woke to the sound of the *Nightwing*'s engine winding up. He wasn't drunk, he hadn't even downed half of the bottle, but he'd had enough to slow his responses. It took him a minute to find his jeans and turn them right-side out. Then two minutes to pull them on—his damn sore leg refusing to cooperate. By the time he'd climbed the stairs, the cruiser was on the move.

The warm night air, when it hit him in the face, took his breath, and Blu felt momentarily dizzy. He blinked and focused, blinked again as his gaze locked on Angel at the helm, her legs planted, her beautiful hair tied back in a long tail that had been cut to fall somewhere in the middle of her back. She was wearing the red-and-purple sarong Lema had given her, and her tiny feet were bare.

For a moment Blu couldn't move, then he limped to the stern and eased down onto the leather bench to watch her handle his boat like a racing pro. He studied her movements as she entered the narrows, watched as she eased off the throttle and maneuvered them through, then suddenly pulled back on the throttle once more and shot them into the Gulf at full speed. Ten minutes later she eased off, then pulled on the wheel and let the cruiser spin into a tricky little circle before bringing her to a gliding halt.

Blu glanced around and saw that she'd brought him to the quiet cove where they had spent half the night driving each other crazy in his bed. His gaze went back to the helm. Waited.

Her shoulders moved up then down as she took a deep breath. Then, slowly, she turned. She didn't say anything at first, simply stood there studying him. Finally she said, "How's your leg and shoulder?"

Blu kept his gaze glued to her. "Fine. How's Mandy?"

"Anxious to see *Da.*"

Her answer threw him, and he sat up a little straighter. "And Perch? How's your grandpa?"

She smiled. "He's been refreshing my memory. I

was a very curious child. By age ten I was driving the pilothouse.''

''So you still don't remember anything?''

''No, not yet. But I'm okay with that for now. Curt— I don't want to remember him. But if and when I do, I'll deal with it.''

''I'm sure you will,'' Blu said, believing it. She was stronger than anyone knew. ''Jackson talk to you? Detail what was in the file?''

''Yes. But I think I would have preferred to hear all of it from you. How long have you known that I was never married to Salva?''

Blu studied her face, listened for the bitterness in her voice. When he didn't hear any, he said, ''I never really knew for sure. It was all speculation. When I learned there was a good chance that Mandy wasn't his, it occurred to me that a man like Maland had no reason to marry someone he already felt he owned.''

''And the reason you didn't tell me days ago?''

''If I told you that, you would have suspected there was more. I promised you that I would keep you safe. Keeping you safe meant I needed to also keep you in the dark, at least until we had Maland baited. You weren't suppose to know what I had planned for Mandy until it was all over.''

''Mort explained how he went to the shelter dressed as me. When I dressed that morning at your mother's place into the disguise you sent with Brodie, I thought the other bag was a disguise for Amanda. Mort made me think she was going to leave the fish market dressed as a boy. But it was Mort's disguise in the bag. Very clever of you.''

''If the wig and makeup worked that day, I knew it would work again at the wharf.''

"And Amanda was the bait?"

Blu looked away. "*Oui,* she was the bait."

"Then it was all about your promise to us? Me and Mandy?"

Blu was only half listening. He couldn't keep going over this. In his mind he had relived that moment a hundred times when Maland's men had drawn their guns. He'd had no right to play God with Mandy's life and he would never forgive himself as long as he lived.

"It's still bothering you—the decision you made—isn't it?"

He turned. "What?"

She closed the distance, came to stand directly in front of him. She looked beautiful against the night sky, her skin so soft, so fragile. "I brought you out here to tell you that I've been waiting every day for you to come home so I could apologize. I came every day to DuBay Pier, and then to River Bay to see if you'd come back. I've been a pest at the fish market. Oh, and I met your sister, and your brother-in-law. They're anxious to have you home, too. Grandpa's been worried I'm going to make myself sick if I don't start eating. And Mort and Brodie—I think they've started to avoid me since the only words I know how to say lately are, 'Have you seen Blu?' And Jackson's no help at all since he's been suspended."

"What's he done this time?"

"Something to do with Salva going into jail in one piece, but ending up with several broken ribs, a broken nose and two black eyes. I guess there are a few other things wrong with him, too."

She was gauging Blu's reaction. He remained sober. "So you're here to apologize? For what?"

"For telling you I hated you. I don't. Never have."

"Okay, so you don't hate me."

"Ah, there's something else, too. I'm here to...to claim what's mine."

Blu came to his feet slowly. "I don't think there's anything of yours left on the boat. At least, I haven't seen anything."

"Oh, but there is." She reached out and laid her hand on his heart. "This— This is mine, isn't it? You gave it to me without telling me days ago. You didn't say the words, but you do love me, don't you, Blu? You love Amanda, too."

"Don't." Blu backed away. "You know who I am, what I've done. You don't want—"

"That's right. I'm no longer naive. I know exactly who you are, and I love who you are."

Blu needed air. But hell, he was standing outside and there was a slight breeze. Still, he felt almost dizzy.

"Breathe, Blu. It helps if you breathe."

He took a solid gulp of air, deciding that was the problem—he'd forgotten to breathe.

"There, that's better." She stepped forward and rubbed his chest, her warm little fingers curling into his flesh. "I saw you. I made Brodie take me to the wharf, and I saw everything. I saw the way you called Salva's attention away from Mort and Amanda. I saw you sacrifice yourself to save them. I saw—"

"Jeez! Brodie was supposed to keep you away until it was all over. I'm sorry. I had no right to play God with Mandy's life. I—"

"Shh. Don't be sorry. We're alive and free because of you. Don't be sorry."

Angry with himself, Blu growled, "Then what the hell should I be?"

She hesitated. Stared up at him a long minute. "Can't you just be...be mine?"

Blu could see tears had entered her eyes. His anger vanished. "Yours?"

"Mmm." She nodded. "Yes, mine. I know I'm really young, and that my memory is still gone for now. But I've been remembering a few things. Grandpa says I've always been an honest person. A hard worker."

Hell, she was trying to sell herself to him. Blu didn't know what to say.

"Grandpa says, dance forward. Don't go backward. He says a man that is good bone-deep is hard to find, and when a woman is lucky enough to find one— Well, I thought maybe we could dance forward together. That's if you—"

"You've talked to Perch about me? About us?"

"Yes. I told him that you and I... We... Say you saved us because you love us, Blu. Say you saved us because you want me."

His hands had started to shake. Blu pulled her into his arms, sighed when her body melted against him. She felt so damn good, he almost forgot what he was going to say. "I want you, *fille.* God, how I want you. It works both ways, though."

"Meaning?"

"What's mine is yours, and what's yours is mine. You know how that old saying goes."

"Yes, I think I know how it goes."

Blu bent his head and kissed her gently, then ran his hand down her back and pressed her against him. "You want to take a ride to heaven?" he asked. "I'll share *mine* if you share *yours.*"

He felt her rub against him, felt her little breathy

sigh escape her lips. On tiptoes, she looked him in the eye, then whispered, "I love you."

"I love you, too." Then he bent his head and kissed her parted lips. "Welcome home, Angel."

Slowly she stepped back and slipped the button through the hole and let the sarong float to the deck. Standing naked in the moonlight, she said, "I've been home for a while. I've decided home is a feeling, not a place. And I've been feeling like I've been home ever since I saw your face in Salva's office. I truly am home, Blu duFray—" she stepped closer and snuggled against him "—and I'm going to stay right here forever."

Epilogue

"He's actually holding her like he knows what he's doing. I can't believe it. If I wasn't standing here—"

"Peeking out the window," Ry pointed out from his position in front of their yellow kitchen stove. He glanced at Kristie, who had volunteered to set the table, and winked.

Kristie smiled, then watched Blu's sister squeeze closer to the window. It was Sunday, and she'd learned that dinner at Margo and Ry's had become a tradition for the Crew, as they called themselves—Blu's family and extended family included Rose and Brodie, Mort and Jackson. And of course, Margo and Ry.

"Margo, I just washed those windows this morning. Your nose is cute, but come on, baby. He's not going to drop her."

"Did I say he was going to drop Mandy?" Margo quickly glanced at Kristie. "He won't, will he?"

"No, he won't drop her," Kristie promised. "Blu wouldn't hurt a fly."

She saw Ry and Margo glance at each other, their expressions both showing concern.

"Maybe I should rephrase that. He wouldn't hurt a fly unless the fly had malicious intent on its mind, with its sights set on one of us."

"Whew! You had us worried for a minute," Margo said.

"I've seen Rose's scrapbook. I know who Patch Pollaro is. More importantly, I know who Blu duFray is." Secretly, Kristie wondered if she was the only one who really did. *Her* Blu was the gentlest man on earth.

"Oh, look. She's leading him over to the swing, Ry. Come look."

Ry stayed where he was at the stove, stirring a mixture that had just started to boil. "Margo, is this supposed to look like this?"

She quickly glanced in his direction. "How should I know? It's a new recipe."

"We're never going to eat unless one of us gets serious here."

"Well, one of us is. And don't you dare let it burn."

"Remember, I don't cook, baby. We've got eight people for dinner and if you leave me in charge, hell, we'll all starve."

"Where's Jackson? Get him in here."

"Somebody call for me?"

From the window Margo said, "Jackson, help Ry. He's burning dinner."

"I am not burning dinner. Not yet, anyway. Here." Kristie watched Ry hand over the spoon to his partner. "It's supposed to be some kind of creole, I think.

There's rice under that cover, and shrimp in the oven. Where did you get that beer?''

''It's on the porch. Brodie brought it.''

''Hewitt's here already?''

''He came with Mort a few minutes ago. Rose is here, too.'' Jackson's gaze found Kristie. ''She came with your grandpa.'' He took a step in her direction and kissed her on the cheek. ''How you doing, sweet thing?''

Kristie blushed. ''I'm doing fine.''

''So the Devil's still treating you all right, or do you need me to take him out behind the house and teach him a lesson or two?''

Laughter came from the window. ''You teach Blu a lesson, ha!'' The laughter grew. ''That, I'd pay to see.''

Ry moved up behind his wife and swatted her small behind. ''Come on, let's get out of here. Kristie, you come, too. Jackson will let us know when dinner's ready.''

Kristie followed both Margo and Ry onto the veranda.

''There you are, Kris.'' Rose appeared and hugged Kristie.

''Hi, Rose. Jackson said you came with Grandpa?''

''Yes. Perch said it was silly for me to take a cab when he was driving right by. Say, Bessy's going to be gone to her sister's next week. Do you think you can help out at the store for a few days?''

''Sure.''

''I could help out.''

Kristie glanced behind her and found her grandpa standing close by. Surprised by his offer, she asked, ''You could?''

"Why not? I know the fishin' business inside and out."

"I would have to agree with that," Rose replied, smiling.

"Then I'll let you two discuss it while I check on my daughter." Kristie stepped off the veranda and crossed the backyard to the swing where Blu sat with Amanda on his lap.

She had selected a light blue sundress to wear to dinner, and had left her hair loose to move against her bare shoulders. There was a gentle breeze, and she could smell jasmine in the air. Blu looked so handsome holding Amanda, his shoes off and his long, jeans-clad legs stretched out in front of him. He looked sinfully sexy and tough as nails. And she was so in love with him that this past week had seemed like a dream.

"Hi, you two."

"Hi, Mommeee." The minute she sat down, Amanda launched herself at Kristie and hugged her, then pointed to Brodie Hewitt, where he stood on the veranda talking to Ry and Margo. "What's dat in Unck's hand?"

"Brodie's thirsty." It was Blu who answered.

"Me firsty, too, Da." Suddenly Amanda wiggled down and set her sights on Brodie. "Unck, me firsty."

She was pointing to his can of beer. Both Blu and Kristie said at the same time, "No!"

Brodie grinned, then moved away from the railing and produced a can from the cooler. Holding it high, he yelled, "I brought Mandy and Rose root beer. Come here, darlin'. Unck will fix you up."

As Amanda trotted off toward the veranda, Kristie felt Blu tug her close and put his arm around her. "So, do you think you're going to like being married to the Crew?"

"Married?" Kristie gazed at him. "What are you saying?"

"Go fishin' in my shirt pocket."

Kristie slipped her hand into the pocket of Blu's sleeveless white T-shirt and when she pulled it out, she was holding a sparkling diamond ring. Blu took it from her, sat up slowly, and slipped it onto her finger. "There."

Kristie glanced at the diamond ring. They hadn't talked about marriage. Oh, she would love to marry Blu. She couldn't think of anything more perfect. Only... "It's beautiful..."

"But?"

"Are you sure you want an instant family so soon? Maybe you should get used to us in small doses for a while. That way if you change your mind—"

"Perch says I can't have you living with me the way things are."

"He what?" Kristie pulled back and frowned. "Is that why you haven't let me stay over on the *Nightwing* this past week?"

"He's right. We should get married."

Kristie was speechless.

"What, you want me on my knee? Is that what you're waiting for?"

"No. Well, not unless you want to."

Blu glanced at the crowd on the veranda. They were all laughing, busy talking. All except Rose and Perch. Blu locked gazes with the old man. Perch smiled, then gave a nod.

His silent approval put Blu on his feet, then down on one knee. Kristie suddenly felt shy. She fidgeted on the swing, straightened her skirt. When she finally looked at Blu, she found him smiling, staring at her mouth. ‘‘What are you looking at?’’

‘‘I sure do love that mouth of yours and how you use it.’’

Kristie blushed. ‘‘Blu, stop teasing.’’

He gestured to his knee. ‘‘Well, here I am. On my bad leg, too. Is this what you want?’’

Kristen shook her head. ‘‘You’re all I want. But I’ll take the Crew, too, if that’s what it takes to spend every night in your arms.’’

He grinned. ‘‘Will you marry me?’’

‘‘In a heartbeat, Blu duFray.’’

The applause from the veranda warned them both that their audience had grown. Blu got to his feet and pulled Kristie off the swing. Then, in front of the Crew—and her grandpa—he kissed *his Angel* like a man in love.

Kristie was still enjoying Blu’s warm lips when Jackson appeared on the veranda and declared dinner was on the table.

* * * * *

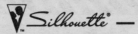